Robinson Crusoe

Robinson Crusoe

Daniel Defoe

Edited by Kathryn Lindskoog
Illustrated by Barbara Chitouras

P&R
PUBLISHING
P.O. BOX 817 • PHILLIPSBURG • NEW JERSEY 08865-0817

**A study guide to this edition
of *Robinson Crusoe* is available
from P&R Publishing
(1 800-631-0094)**

Library of Congress Cataloging-in-Publication Data

Defoe, Daniel, 1661?–1731.
    Robinson Crusoe / Daniel Defoe ; edited by Kathryn Lindskoog ;
illustrated by Barbara Chitouras.
        p. cm — (Classics for young readers)
    Originally published: Portland, Ore. : Multnomah, 1991.
    Summary: As the sole survivor of a shipwreck, and Englishman lives
for nearly thirty years on a deserted island.
    ISBN-10: 0-87552-735-3
    ISBN-13: 978-0-87552-735-2
    [1. Shipwrecks—Fiction. 2. Survival—Fiction.] I. Lindskoog, Kathryn
Ann. II. Chitouras, Barbara, ill. III. Title. IV. Series.

PZ7.D36 Ro 2002
[Fic]—dc21
                                                                    2002028541

CONTENTS

1
THE FAMILY LEFT BEHIND

I WAS BORN IN 1632, in York, England, of a good family. My father was a successful merchant who retired to York, where he married my mother. My mother's family was named Robinson (a good family in that country), and so I was named Robinson Kreutznaer. But we now call ourselves and write our name *Crusoe*, and so my companions always called me.

I had two older brothers. One was lieutenant-colonel to an English regiment and was killed at the battle near Dunkirk against the Spaniards. What became of my second brother I never knew—any more than my father and mother ever knew what became of me.

Being the third son of the family, and not trained for any trade, my head began to be filled with rambling thoughts. My father, who was very old, had planned for me to study law. But I would be satisfied with nothing but going to sea. I went so strongly against the will of my father and all the begging of my mother and other friends that it was as if I was drawn to the life of misery which awaited me.

My father, a wise man, called me one morning into his room, where he was in bed with gout. He asked me why I would leave my father's house and my native country, where I had opportunity for earning a life of ease and pleasure. He told me it was for desperately poor men or for men of great wealth to go abroad on adventures. I was neither poor nor wealthy, which my father had found by long experience was the best state in the world, the most suited to human happiness—not exposed to the miseries and hardships of the poor of mankind, and not embarrassed with the pride, luxury, ambition, and envy of the rich of mankind. He told me that kings have frequently wished they had been placed in the middle of the two extremes, and the wise man prays to have neither poverty nor riches.

He told me I would always find that most calamities in life were shared by the rich and the poor, but that those in the middle had the fewest disasters. Either luxury and extravagance or hard labor and insufficient diet bring unhappiness, but the happy medium provided all kind of virtues and enjoyments—peace and plenty, health and friendship. This way people can go smoothly through the world and comfortably out of it, not sold to a life of slavery for daily bread or harassed by envy and ambition for great things.

After this, he begged me, with much affection, not to cast myself into miseries I was not born into. I had no need to seek hard work; he would find me a good occupation. He would do kind things for me if I would stay and settle at home as he directed. But he had reasoned the same way with my brother—who had run off to war anyway, where he was killed. Though he said he always would pray for me, yet if I did take this foolish step, God would not bless me. I would later have a long time to regret that I rejected his advice, with no one to help me.

This was truly prophetic, though my father did not know it. I observed the tears run down his face, especially when he spoke of my brother who was killed. When he spoke of my having a long time to repent, his heart was so full he could say no more.

I was moved by his talk—who wouldn't have been?—and I resolved not to think of going abroad any more, but to settle at home according to my father's desire.

But within a few days it all wore off, and in a few weeks I resolved to run away. One day when I thought my mother a little more pleasant

"That boy might be happy if he would stay at home, but if he goes abroad he will be the most miserable man that was ever born."

9

than ordinary, I told her I was determined to see the world and wanted my father to give me his permission. I was now eighteen years old, and if she would ask my father to let me go on one voyage abroad and I found I did not like it, I would go no more, and I would promise to work twice as hard to make up for lost time.

This greatly upset my mother. She wondered how I could think of any such thing after the talk with my father, and such kind and tender expressions as she knew my father had used with me. If I was going to ruin myself, I could be sure I would never have their permission. She would take no part in my destruction, and I would never be able to say that my mother was willing when my father was not.

I learned later that she reported the conversation to my father, and he said to her with a sigh, "That boy might be happy if he would stay at home, but if he goes abroad he will be the most miserable man that was ever born. I cannot agree to it."

It was not till almost a year after this that I broke loose, though in the meantime I refused to listen to all proposals of settling down to business, and frequently complained to my father and mother about their being so set against what they knew I wanted. But one day I was at the seaport of Hull, with no intention of running away, and one of my companions invited me to go with him to London in his father's ship, with the allurement that it would cost me nothing. I agreed to go without consulting either my father or mother or even sending them a message, without asking God's blessing or my father's, without any thought of the consequences—and it was a foolish choice, God knows.

2
FIRST ADVENTURES AT SEA

ON THE FIRST OF SEPTEMBER, 1651, I went on board a ship bound for London. Never did any young adventurer's misfortunes begin sooner or continue longer than mine. The wind began to blow and the waves to rise in a most frightful manner, and as I had never been at sea before, I was sick and terrified. I began seriously to think about my wickedness in leaving my father's house, and abandoning my duty. All the good counsel of my parents, my father's tears and my mother's pleadings, came fresh into my mind.

The storm increased, and I expected every wave to swallow us up. Every time the ship dropped down in a trough of the sea, I thought we would never rise again. In this agony of mind I made many vows and resolutions. If God would spare my life and I got my foot upon dry land again, I would never set it into a ship as long as I lived. I saw clearly the goodness of my father's advice, and I resolved that I would, like a true repenting prodigal, go home to him.

These wise thoughts continued all the while the storm continued, but the next day it calmed down. The sun went down perfectly clear and rose clear the next morning. I thought the sun shining on a smooth sea was the most delightful that I ever saw.

I had slept well in the night and was no longer seasick, looking with wonder upon the sea that could quickly become so calm and so pleasant.

My friend came to me, clapping me on the shoulder, and said, "Well, Bob, how are you doing now? I'm sure you were frightened, but we think nothing of a squall like that. Let's make a bowl of punch and forget about it."

To make short this sad part of my story, we went the old way of sailors—the punch was made, and I got drunk and drowned all my repentance and all my resolutions. When the vows and promises tried to return to my mind, I shook them off by drinking again. I had in five or six days got as complete a victory over conscience as any young fellow could desire. But the next storm was worse.

Our sixth day at sea we had to harbor with several other ships, and here we lay for seven or eight days waiting for a good wind. The morning of the eighth day the wind increased, and we had all hands at work to lower our topmasts and make everything snug and tight.

By this time a terrible storm blew in. As the captain went by my cabin, I could hear him say softly to himself several times, "Lord be merciful to us. We shall all be lost!" I was dreadfully frightened, and got up and looked out. I never saw a more dismal sight—the sea went mountains high and broke upon us every three or four minutes. Our men cried out that a ship about a mile ahead of us was sunk. Two more ships, torn from their anchors, were washed out to sea without a mast standing.

Toward evening the mate and boatswain begged the master of our ship to let them cut away the foremast, which he was unwilling to do. Finally he consented, and when they had cut away the foremast, the mainmast stood so loose and shook the ship so much, they were obliged to cut her away also, and make a clear deck.

The storm was so violent that I saw what is not often seen—the master, the boatswain, and some others more sensible than the rest, praying and expecting every moment that the ship would go to the bottom. In the middle of the night, one of the men cried out we had sprung a leak. Another said there was four feet of water in the hold.

The men told me that I, though able to do nothing before, was well able to pump, so I went to the pump and worked as hard as I could. While this was going on, the master ordered gunfire as a signal of distress. I was so surprised that I thought the ship had broken, and I fainted. Another man stepped up to the pump and shoved me aside with his foot, thinking I was dead. It was a long time before I came to.

We worked on, but it was apparent the ship would sink. So the master continued firing guns for help, and a light ship sent a boat out to help us. It was with the greatest hazard the boat came near us, but it was impossible for us to get on board. At last our men cast over the stern a rope with a buoy attached, which they managed to grab hold of, and we hauled them close to our stern and all got into their boat. It was useless for them to try to return to their own ship, so partly rowing and partly drifting, our boat went north toward the shore.

We were not much more than a quarter of an hour out of our ship when we saw her sink. When our boat mounted the waves, we were able to see a great many people running along the shore to help us, but we couldn't get to shore there. Eventually we got safely to shore farther north, and walked on foot to Yarmouth. There the town gave us good lodging and enough money for each of us to go on to London or to return to Hull.

Had I had the sense to go home, I would have been happy. And my father, like the father in our Savior's parable, would have killed the fatted calf for me, for he heard that my ship went down, and he did not know if I had drowned.

At Yarmouth my friend explained to his father that this was my first sample of life at sea, and he said to me solemnly, "Young man, you ought never to go to sea again. You ought to take this for a plain and visible token that you are not to be a seafaring man."

"Why, sir," I said, "won't you go to sea anymore?"

"That is another case," he said. "It is my calling and therefore my duty. Perhaps this has all happened to us on your account, like Jonah in the ship of Tarsus." After I told him some of my story, he burst out, "What have I done that such a wretch should come on my ship? I would not set my foot in the same ship with you again for a thousand pounds." He begged me to go back to my father and not tempt Providence. "And, young man," he said, "depend upon it—if you do not go back, wherever you go you will meet with nothing but disasters and disappointments, till your father's words are fulfilled."

I didn't answer much, and what became of him I don't know. As for me, having some money in my pocket, I traveled to London by land and had many struggles with myself whether I should go home or go to sea.

It occurred to me that I would be laughed at by the neighbors, and would be ashamed to see my father and mother and everybody else. Many people like me are not ashamed to sin, and yet are ashamed to repent; not ashamed to act like fools, but ashamed to act wise and set things right.

That evil influence, whatever it was that made me deaf to all good advice and to the command of my father, caused me to make a terrible choice. I decided to go on board a vessel bound for the coast of Africa (or, as our sailors commonly call it, a voyage to Guinea).

I was befriended by a captain who had made money on the coast of Guinea, and who was resolved to go again. He took a liking to me, and because I wanted see the world, he offered to take me along at no expense. I would eat my meals with him and be his companion, and if I could sell merchandise in Africa, I might make a good profit.

I went with him, and with his help I profited, for I carried about forty pounds worth of such toys and trifles as he told me to buy. This money I had borrowed by mail from some of my relatives, and I believe they got my father, or at least my mother, to contribute.

This was the only successful voyage in all my adventures, thanks to the integrity and honesty of my friend the captain—who taught me mathematics, the rules of navigation, how to keep an account of the ship's course, and how to take an observation. As he took delight to teach me, I took delight to learn, and this voyage made me both a sailor and a merchant. I brought home five pounds nine ounces of gold dust, which yielded me in London at my return almost three hundred pounds, and this filled me with the ambition that completed my ruin.

Yet even in this voyage I had my misfortunes. I was continually sick from the excessive heat of the climate near the equator.

3

IN AND OUT OF SLAVERY

I HAD NOW BECOME A TRADER, though to my great misfortune, my friend died. So I set sail with the new captain of his ship. Though I did not carry quite a hundred pounds of my new-gained wealth, so that I had two hundred pounds left which I entrusted to my friend's widow, yet I fell into terrible misfortunes in this voyage.

Between the Canary Islands and the African shore, our ship was surprised in the gray of the morning by Turkish pirates from Sallee. They gave chase, and we prepared to fight, our ship having twelve guns and their ship eighteen. About three in the afternoon they caught up with us, and we poured in a broadside upon them, which made them sheer off again, after returning our fire and pouring in also his small-arms fire from the nearly two hundred men he had on board. The next time he attacked, he entered sixty men upon our decks, who immediately began cutting and hacking the decks and rigging. With our ship disabled and three of our men killed and eight wounded, we had to yield, and were carried as prisoners into Sallee, a port belonging to the Moors.

The treatment we received was not as dreadful as I first feared, nor was I carried away to the Emperor of Morocco as the rest of our men were, but was kept by the pirate captain as his prize slave, being young and able. I was overwhelmed by this surprising change of my circumstances from a merchant to a miserable slave, and now I recalled my father's warning to me. This was but a taste of the misery I was to go through, as will appear later in my story.

I hoped my new master would take me with him when he went to sea again. I believed that at some time or other he would be defeated and I would again be free. But when he went to sea, he left me on shore to look after his little garden and do the common toil of slaves. When he came home again from his cruise, he ordered me to stay in the cabin to look after the ship. I could find no way to escape.

Once or twice a week in fair weather my master would take the ship's rowboat and go fishing. He always took me and a boy named Xury with him to row the boat. We made him merry, and I proved skillful in catching fish—so much so that sometimes he would send me and Xury with a relative of his named Ismael to catch a dish of fish for him.

It happened that, going fishing in a stark calm morning, a fog rose so thick that though we were not half a league from the shore, we lost sight of it and rowed the wrong direction. We were at sea all day and all night and very hungry. Our master resolved to take more care of himself in the future, and instructed another English slave to build a little cabin on a captured sailboat. In the cabin there was room to sleep, a little table, and lockers with bread, rice, and coffee. We went out frequently on this new fishing barge, and my master never went without me.

One time he decided to take some important guests out and had the boat stocked with food and gunpowder for shooting seabirds. I got everything ready as he had directed and waited the next morning with the boat washed clean, but his guests had to postpone the outing. He ordered me to go out anyway and catch some fish for dinner.

This was my chance to escape.

I told Ismael that we must not use the food for guests, so he brought a large basket of biscuits and three jars with fresh water. I knew where my master's case of bottles stood, stolen from some English ship, and I secretly stashed them on the boat.

I also took a great lump of beeswax, with a parcel of string, a hatchet, a saw, and a hammer, all which were of great use to us afterwards, especially the wax to make candles. I told Ismael that the guns were on board the boat and that if he would get a little powder and shot we might kill some birds for ourselves. So he brought ammunition, and I was able to sneak some gunpowder on board in a bottle.

Thus we sailed out of the port to fish. The port guards knew who we were and took no notice of us. We were not more than a mile out of the port before we hauled in our sail and began to fish. We caught nothing, for when I had a fish on my hook I would not pull it in. I said to Ismael, "This will not do. We must go out farther." Ismael agreed and set the sails. When we were out far enough, I stepped forward to where he was, and pretending to stoop for something behind him, I took him by surprise and tossed him overboard.

He rose immediately, for he swam like a cork, and swam so strong after the boat that he would have reached us quickly. I stepped into the cabin, grabbed one of the guns, and pointed it at him. "You swim well enough to reach the shore, and the sea is calm. Make your way to shore and I will do you no harm. But if you come near the boat, I'll shoot you, for I am going to get my liberty." So he turned himself about and swam for the shore, and I have no doubt he reached it with ease.

I said to the boy, "Xury, if you will be faithful to me I'll make you a great man. If you will not, I must throw you into the sea too." The boy smiled and swore to be faithful to me and go all over the world with me.

I headed out to sea to fool Ismael. But as soon as dusk came, I changed my course and steered southeast, bending my course a little toward the east, in order to keep close to the shore. Having a fair, fresh wind and a smooth, quiet sea, I made such good headway that I believed by the next day at three o'clock in the afternoon, when I first went ashore, I could not be less than 150 miles south of Sallee.

I did not stop for five days, and then I concluded that if any of the Moorish vessels were chasing me, they would now give up. So I anchored in the mouth of a little river, I knew not what or where. I neither saw or desired to see any people. The principal thing I wanted was fresh water. As soon as it was dark we heard such dreadful barking, roaring, and howling of wild creatures that poor Xury was ready to die with fear.

The next day we waded to shore, carrying nothing but our guns and two jars for water. I did not want to lose sight of the boat, fearing the coming of canoes with savages down the river. But the boy walked inland, and by and by he came running toward me with something hanging over his shoulders, which was an animal he had shot, like a hare, which was very good meat. But the great joy Xury came with was to tell me he had found good water, and had seen no wild men.

By the best of my calculation, that place must be the country which lies uninhabited except by wild beasts—tigers, lions, leopards, and other furious creatures—so that the Moors use it for their hunting only, where they go like an army, two or three thousand men at a time. For nearly a hundred miles along the coast we saw nothing but an uninhabited country by day and heard nothing but the howling and roaring of wild beasts by night.

Several times I had to send Xury inland for fresh water. Once we anchored under a little point of land where Xury saw a huge, sleeping lion by the shore. We used all three of our guns to finish him off. I was sorry to lose three charges of powder and shot upon a creature that was good for nothing to us. I thought, however, that perhaps the skin might be of some value to us, so Xury and I went to work on him. It took us the whole day, but at last we got the hide off him and spread it on the top of our cabin to dry in the sun. It afterwards served me to lie upon.

After this stop we headed southward for ten or twelve days, going to shore only as often as needed for fresh water. I knew that all the ships from Europe which sailed to the coast of Guinea or to Brazil or to the East Indies came near here, and if we didn't meet with some ship we would perish.

In two or three places, as we sailed by, we saw dark, naked people looking at us from the shore. I kept at a distance, but talked with them by signs as well as I could, and particularly made signs for something to eat. They beckoned to me to stop my boat, and that they would bring me some meat. I lowered the top of my sail and waited, and two of them ran up into the country. In less than half-an-hour they were back, and brought with them two pieces of dried meat and some grain. They brought it to the shore and laid it down, then stood at a distance until we brought it on board, when they came close to us again.

We made signs of thanks to them, for we had nothing to give them. Suddenly two mighty leopards rushed from the mountains toward the sea, and the people were terribly frightened. I had loaded my gun and told Xury to load both the others. As soon as one of the beasts came near, I shot him. Immediately he sank into the water, but rose instantly, and plunged up and down, struggling for life. He died just before he reached the shore, and the second leopard ran back to the mountains.

It is impossible to express the astonishment of the people at the noise and flash of my gun. They offered me some of the leopard's meat, which I declined, but I made signs for the skin, which they gave me freely and also brought me more of their food. Then I made signs to them for some water. They called to some of their friends, and two women brought a large pot, which they set down for me as before. I sent Xury on shore to fill our three jars.

I was now furnished with roots, grain, and water, and I sailed on for about eleven more days without going near the shore. Suddenly, Xury cried out, "Master, master, a ship with a sail!" He was frightened out of his wits, thinking it was some of his master's ships. I saw, however, that it was a Portuguese ship, and thought it was bound for the coast of Guinea to pick up slaves. Instead, they were headed out to sea.

Fortunately, they saw with the help of their spyglasses that our boat was European, which, as they supposed, must belong to some ship that was lost. So they shortened sail to let me come out to meet them. I signaled distress and in about three hours' time I reached them.

They asked me where I was from in Portuguese, in Spanish, and in French, but I understood none of them. At last a Scottish sailor on board called to me, and I told him I was an Englishman and had made my escape out of slavery from the Moors, at Sallee. Then they invited me on board and kindly took me in.

I offered all I had to the captain of the ship, as a return for my deliverance. But he generously told me he would take nothing from me. "For I would be glad to be saved myself, and I may at some time or other need rescuing. Besides, when I carry you to Brazil, if I should take from you what you have, you will starve there, and then I only take away that life I have given. No, Mr. Englishman, I will carry you there free, so that you may go home again."

4
FROM BRAZIL TO A SHIPWRECK

THE CAPTAIN DID WHAT HE SAID—he took everything of mine and gave me an exact inventory so that I might have it all back, even down to the three pottery jars.

My boat was a good one, and he told me he would buy it for the ship's use, and asked me what I would take for it. I told him he had been so generous to me that I could not request any price for the boat, but left the amount entirely to him. He told me he would pay me eighty pieces of eight in Brazil, and if any one offered me more, he would make up the difference. He also offered me sixty pieces of eight for Xury, which I hated to take because I hated to sell the poor boy's liberty, who had helped me so faithfully in restoring my own. When I told the captain my reason, he promised to set the boy free in ten years if he became a Christian. When Xury said he was willing to go with him, I let the captain have him.

We had a good voyage to Brazil and arrived in All Saints' Bay in about twenty-two days.

The generous captain refused to let me pay for my passage, and gave me twenty ducats for the leopard's skin and forty for the lion's skin. What I was willing to sell he bought, such as the case of bottles, two of my guns, and a piece of the lump of beeswax (I had made candles of the rest). Altogether I made about 220 pieces of eight from all my cargo, and with this I went on shore in Brazil.

I lived for awhile at a sugar plantation, and seeing that the planters grew rich, I resolved, if I could get a license to settle there, I would do the same. I hoped to get the money I had left in London. In the meantime, I purchased as much land as I could and planned a plantation.

A man named Wells had a plantation next to mine. We planted food for about two years. Then in the third year we planted some tobacco and got ready to plant sugar cane the following year. But we both needed help, and now I realized how wrong I had been in parting with my helper Xury.

For me to do wrong was no great wonder. I had chosen a career the opposite of what I enjoy, after leaving my father's house and ignoring all his good advice. Now I was aiming at the kind of life my father recommended, and I might as well have stayed at home. I often said to myself, "I could just as well have done this in England among my friends as have gone five thousand miles to do it among strangers and savages."

I had nobody to talk with, except Wells now and then. If any work was to be done, it was by the labor of my hands. I complained that I lived just like a man cast away upon some desolate island, with nobody there but himself. (When people liken their present conditions to others that are worse, heaven may switch them over so they realize the difference the hard way.)

My kind friend, the captain of the ship that rescued me, was going back to Portugal. When I told him I had left money behind in London, he offered to bring it to me in Brazil if I would make out papers for him. He advised me to send for only a hundred pounds and to leave the other hundred in London.

I wrote the English captain's widow a full account of all my adventures—my slavery, escape, and how I had met with the Portuguese captain at sea, and his kind behavior. When she heard this, she not only followed my directions, but out of her own pocket sent the captain a handsome present for his humanity and charity to me.

The captain brought a hundred pounds worth of goods to me in Brazil, including tools, iron-work, and utensils necessary for my plantation. These were of great use to me. When this cargo arrived, I thought my fortune made. The captain had even spent the five pounds my friend had sent him for a present, to purchase me a bondservant obligated for six years' service. Furthermore, English products such as cloth were valuable in Brazil, so I made a large profit, and I bought myself a Negro slave and another European servant.

But prosperity is oftentimes our downfall. I had great success with my plantation the next year, and with the increased business and wealth, my head began to be full of projects and undertakings beyond my reach. Just as I had once left my parents behind, now I could not be content to be a rich and thriving man in my new plantation.

I had now lived almost four years in Brazil and had not only learned the language, but had made friends among my fellow-planters and the merchants of San Salvador. I had told about my two voyages to the coast of Guinea and how easy it was to purchase for trifles—such as beads, toys, knives, scissors, hatchets, bits of glass, and the like—not only such items as gold dust and elephants' teeth, but also Negroes to work as slaves.

Three of them came to me one morning to make a secret proposal. They wanted to send a ship to Guinea to bring back slaves for their plantations, and if I would go to do the trading, they would give me some of the slaves. With my flourishing plantation and the money I had in England, I could easily have been worth three or four thousand pounds sterling in three or four years. To think of such a voyage was the most preposterous thing a person in my circumstances could do.

But I, as if born to be my own destroyer, could no more resist the offer than I could restrain my early desire to go to sea. I told them I would go, and I made out my will. I went on board September 1,

1659, eight years after I first sailed from Hull.

We set sail, meaning to head north up the coast of Brazil, then cross the Atlantic to Africa. But after about twelve days' time, a violent hurricane sent us scudding away before it, wherever fate and the fury of the winds directed, for twelve days.

In this distress we had, besides the terror of the storm, one of our men die of the fever, and one man and boy washed overboard. We were far from civilization and knew we could not possibly make our voyage to Africa without some assistance, both to our ship and to ourselves.

Then a second storm came upon us, which carried us away again. Early in the morning one of our men cried out, "Land!" We had no sooner run out of our cabin to look out, in hopes of seeing where in the world we were, but the ship struck upon a sandbar. The sea broke over her so forcefully we expected the ship to break in pieces and us to perish.

In this distress, the mate of our vessel took hold of the small boat on our deck, and with the help of the rest of the men, got it slung over the ship's side. We all got into it, let go, and committed ourselves, being eleven in number, to God's mercy and the wild sea.

Now we all saw plainly that the waves were so high that the boat could not survive, and we would be drowned. So we rowed toward the sand, though with heavy hearts, like men going to their execution, for we all knew that when the boat came nearer the shore, it would be dashed in a thousand pieces. However, we earnestly committed our souls to God and, with the wind driving us toward the shore, hastened our destruction with our own hands by pulling as well as we could toward land.

As we came nearer and nearer the shore, the land looked more frightful than the sea. After we had gone about a league and a half, a raging, mountain-like wave came rolling up behind us, and took us with such a fury that it overturned the boat. We were separated from

26

the boat as well as from one another, and had no time to cry, "O God!" for we were all swallowed up in a moment.

That wave carried me a long way toward the shore, and having spent itself, went back and left me almost upon dry land, though half dead with the water I took in. I got up and struggled toward the land as fast as I could, before another wave overtook me. But I soon found it was impossible to avoid it. I saw the sea come after me as high as a great hill, and as furious as an enemy. My greatest concern was that the wave, which would carry me a great way towards the shore when it came in, would carry me back again when it went out to sea.

The wave that came upon me buried me in twenty or thirty feet of water, and I could feel myself carried with a mighty force and swiftness toward the shore. I held my breath and swam forward with all my might. I was ready to burst with holding my breath, when, as I felt myself rising up, to my immediate relief I found my head and hands shoot out above the surface of the water. Though I was not out of the water more than two seconds, it was a great relief and gave me breath and new courage. I was covered again with water a good while but was able to hold out. Once the water had spent itself and began to return, I pushed against the return of the waves and felt the ground again with my feet. I stood still a few moments to recover my breath and let the water recede, and then ran with what strength I had toward the shore. Yet even this did not deliver me from the fury of the sea, which came pouring in after me again. Twice more I was lifted up by the waves and carried forward as before, the shore being very flat.

The last of these two waves was nearly fatal to me, for it dashed me against a piece of a rock with such force that it left me senseless and helpless to deliver myself. The blow knocked the breath out of me, and had it returned immediately, I would have drowned. But I recovered a little before the next wave, and when I saw I would be covered again with water, I resolved to hang on to a piece of the rock and to hold my breath, if possible, till the wave went back. The waves were not as high as at first, since I was closer to land. I held on till the wave had spent itself and then ran again, which brought me so near the shore that the next wave, though it went over me, did not swallow me up and carry me away. With my next run I got to the mainland, where to my great comfort I clambered up the cliffs of the shore and sat on the grass, free from danger and out of reach of the water.

I was now safe on shore and began to look up and thank God that my life was saved where a few minutes before there was scarce any room to hope. It is impossible to express the ecstasies and transports of the soul when it is saved out of the very grave. I walked about on the shore, lifting up my hands and my whole being, wrapped up in the contemplation of my deliverance, making a thousand gestures and motions which I cannot describe, reflecting upon all my comrades who were drowned, and that I should be the only one saved. I never saw any sign of the other men except three of their hats, one cap, and an unmatched pair of shoes.

I looked toward the stranded vessel and could hardly see it, it lay so far off, and considered, *Lord! how was it possible I could get on shore?*

After I had calmed my mind with the comfortable part of my condition, I began to look around to see what kind of place I was in and what to do next. My comforts soon faded, for I was wet, had no other clothes, nor anything to eat or drink. I saw no other prospect before me but to perish with hunger or be devoured by wild beasts. What was particularly afflicting to me was that I had no weapon either to hunt and kill any creature for food or to defend myself against any other creature that might desire to kill me for theirs. I had nothing about me but a knife, a pipe, and a little tobacco in a box. This was all my provision, and this threw me into such terrible distress that for a while I ran about like a madman. With night coming upon me, I began, with a heavy heart, to consider what would happen to me if there were any ravenous beasts in that country, since they always come abroad for their prey at night.

The only remedy I could think of was to get up into a thick, bushy tree like a fir, but thorny, which grew near me. I resolved to sit there all night and consider the next day what death I would die, for as yet I saw no prospect of life. I walked about a furlong from the shore to see if I could find any fresh water to drink, which I did, to my great joy. I then went to the tree, and getting up into it, tried to place myself so that if I fell asleep I would not fall. Having cut a short stick, like a club, for my defense, I took up my lodging. I fell fast asleep and slept as comfortably as, I believe, few could have done in my condition.

5
LOOTING THE WRECKED SHIP

WHEN I AWOKE it was broad day. The weather was clear and the storm abated, so the sea did not rage and swell as before. What surprised me most was that the tide had lifted the ship off the sandbar in the night, and she had been swept in almost as far as the rock where I had been so bruised by the wave dashing me against it. This was within about a mile from shore, and the ship was still upright.

When I came down from my apartment in the tree, the first thing I found was the small boat, which lay as the wind and the sea had tossed it upon the sand about two miles away. I soon found that there was an inlet about half a mile wide blocking my way, and I decided to try to reach the ship first, in search of provisions.

A little after noon the sea was calm, and the tide ebbed so far out that I could walk within a quarter mile of the ship. This increased my grief, for I saw that if we had stayed on board we all would have made it safe to shore, and I would not be left here miserably alone. I wept again, but as there was little relief in that, I resolved, if possible, to get to the ship. I pulled off most of my clothes, for the weather was extremely hot, and took to the water. But when I came to the ship there was nothing within my reach to take hold of. I swam around her twice, and the second time I spied a small piece of a rope, which I was surprised I had not seen at first, hanging down by the fore-chains so that with great difficulty I got hold of it, and by the help of that rope got into the forecastle of the ship. I found that all the ship's food was dry and untouched by the water. Being eager to eat, I went to the breadroom and filled my pockets with biscuits and ate as I went about other things, for I had no time to lose. I wished I had a boat to carry to shore the many things I would need.

I flung a spare topmast and some other pieces of wood overboard, tying each one with a rope so it wouldn't drift away. When this was done I went down the ship's side, and pulling them to me, I tied four of them together at both ends as well as I could, in the form of a raft, then added more wood. With the carpenter's saw I cut a spare topmast into three lengths, and added them, with a great deal of hard work.

My raft was now strong enough to bear any reasonable weight. I first laid all the planks or boards upon it that I could, then took three of the seamen's chests I had broken open and emptied and lowered them onto my raft. The first of these I filled with bread, rice, three Dutch cheeses, five pieces of dried goat's meat, and a little remainder of European corn which had been food for some fowl we brought to sea with us, but the birds were killed. There had been some barley and wheat, but to my great disappointment, I found that the rats had eaten or spoiled it all. While I did all this, the tide was calmly rising, and I looked up and saw my coat, shirt, and waistcoat, which I had left on the shore, float away. I went rummaging for clothes, of which I found enough, but took no more than I wanted for present use. After long searching I found the carpenter's chest, which was much more valuable than a shipload of gold. I put it on my raft without taking time to look into it, for I knew in general what it contained. Next I added some ammunition, four guns, and a couple of rusty swords.

Now I began to think how I should get my raft to shore, having only a couple of broken oars. But I had three encouragements: A smooth, calm sea, the rising tide, and a slight breeze blowing me toward the land. It was an extremely difficult trip, and I almost lost my cargo a couple of times, but in the end, by taking advantage of the tide, I got my raft and all my cargo safely on shore.

Where I was, I did not know—whether on the continent or on an island, whether inhabited or uninhabited, whether in danger of wild beasts or not. There was a hill, not more than a mile from me, which rose up steep and high. After I had with great difficulty climbed to the top, I saw my fate: I was on an island surrounded by sea, with two smaller islands about three leagues to the west.

The island I was on was barren and seemed uninhabited except by animals. I saw only unfamiliar birds. It took me the rest of that day to unload the raft. At night I barricaded myself with the chests and boards I had brought on shore, and made a kind of a hut.

I realized I should get everything possible out of the ship and debated whether I should take back the raft. But I decided to go as before, when the tide was down, and I did so, only I stripped before I went from my hut, having nothing on but a checkered shirt, a pair of linen pants, and a pair of shoes.

I got on board the ship as before and prepared a second raft. Having had experience with the first, I made this one smaller and did not overload it, though I brought away tools, including a grindstone. All these I secured, together with several things belonging to the gunner. Besides these things, I took all the men's clothes I could find, and a spare fore-top sail, a hammock, and some bedding. With this I loaded my second raft, and brought them all safely to shore, to my great comfort.

When I came back, I found no sign of any visitor. But sitting on one of the chests was a creature like a wild cat which, when I came toward it, ran away a little distance and then stood still. I tossed her a bit of biscuit, and she went to it, smelled it, ate it, and looked for more. But I could spare no more, so she marched off.

I went to work to make me a little tent with the sail and some poles

After I had with great difficulty climbed to the top, I saw my fate:
I was on an island surrounded by sea . . .

which I cut for that purpose. Into this tent I brought everything that I knew would spoil either from rain or sun, and I piled all the empty chests and casks up in a circle around the tent, to fortify it from attack. Spreading one of the beds on the ground, laying my two pistols at my head, and my gun at length by me, I went to bed for the first time and slept quietly all night, for I was exhausted.

Every day at low water I went on board and brought away something or other. The third time I went I brought away as much of the rigging as I could, and also all the small ropes and twine I could get, and a piece of spare canvas, which was used to mend the sails. And I cut up the sails, for they were no more use as sails, but they were strong canvas.

After five or six trips, I found a great hogshead of bread, a box of sugar, and a barrel of fine flour. I wrapped up the bread parcel by parcel in pieces of the sails, and I got all this safely to shore also.

The next day I made another voyage. Now, having plundered the ship of what was portable, I began with the cables. I cut the great cable into pieces I could move, I got two cables and a hawser on shore, and took some heavy iron-work—much of which I lost, because the raft tipped over. I went every day, and brought away what I could.

I had now been on shore thirteen days and had been on board the ship eleven times. In this time I had brought away all that any two hands could bring, though I believe if the calm weather had held, I would have brought away the whole ship piece by piece. I thought I had rummaged the cabin so carefully that nothing more could be found, yet I discovered a locker with drawers in it, in which I found two or three razors and a pair of large scissors, a dozen or so good knives and forks, some European and Brazilian coins, and some gold and silver. I smiled to myself at the sight of so much money. "O drug!" said I aloud, "what are you good for? One knife is worth more than all this pile of money."

I began to think about making another raft, but then noticed the sky was overcast and the wind was beginning to rise. It occurred to me that I'd better leave, otherwise I might not be able to reach the shore at all. So I lowered myself into the water and swam to shore with difficulty, partly from the weight of the things I was carrying and partly the roughness of the water in the rising gale.

But I made it home to my little tent, where I lay with all my wealth about me very secure. It blew hard all that night, and in the morning, when I looked out, no more ship was to be seen.

I resolved to find a better spot of ground for my little home. I wanted good drainage and fresh water, shelter from the heat of the sun, security from enemies, whether men or animals, and a view of the sea, so that if God sent any ship my way I would not miss a chance of rescue, of which I was not willing to give up hope yet.

In my search for a better place, I found a little plain on the side of a rising hill. The face of the hill above this plain was as steep as the side of a house, so that nothing could come down upon me from the top. On the side of this rock there was a hollow place, worn a little way in, like the entrance or door of a cave. But there was not really any cave, or way into the rock at all.

On the flat of the green, just before this hollow place, I decided to pitch my tent. This plain was not more than a hundred yards wide and about twice as long, and lay like a green before my door, and at the end of it descended irregularly every way down into the low grounds by the seaside. It was on the northwest side of the hill so that I was sheltered from the heat of the sun until late evening.

Before I set up my tent, I drew a half circle in front of the hollow place, extending about ten yards out from the rock. In this half circle I pitched two rows of strong stakes, driving them into the ground till they stood firm, out of the ground about five-and-a-half feet, and sharpened on the top. The two rows were no more than six inches from one another.

Then I took the pieces of cable I had cut in the ship and laid them in rows one upon another, between these two rows of stakes, up to the top. I placed other stakes in the inside leaning against them, about two-and-a-half feet high, like a spur to a post. This fence was so strong that neither man nor beast could get into it or over it. This cost me much time and labor, especially to cut the stakes, bring them to the place, and drive them into the earth.

I made the entrance into this place not by a door but by a short ladder, to go over the top. When I was inside, I lifted the ladder over after me, and so I was completely fenced in and fortified, as I thought, from all the world. I slept secure at night, which otherwise I could not have done, though, as it appeared afterwards, there was no need of all this caution.

6
MAKING A HOME

INTO THIS FORTRESS I carried all my riches. I also made a large tent with a smaller tent within, to protect me from the rains that in one part of the year are violent there. I slept now in a hammock, a very good one that had belonged to the mate of the ship.

I next gathered rocks and laid them up within my fence in the nature of a terrace, and I made a cave just behind my tent, which served me like a cellar or a kitchen.

One day, before I had finished all this, there was a heavy rainstorm with lightning and thunder. A thought darted into my mind as swift as the lightning itself. My gunpowder! My heart sank within me when I thought that at one blast all my powder could be destroyed, on which my defense and my food entirely depended. I was never so anxious about my own danger, though had the powder exploded, I would not have known what hit me.

After the storm was over, I set aside all my building and fortifying and applied myself to make bags and boxes to separate about 240 pounds of powder into a hundred little parcels, in hope that it would never all ignite at once. I finished this work in about two weeks. As to the barrel that had been wet, I was not in any danger from that, so I placed it in my new cave. The rest I hid in holes among the rocks, so that none of it would get wet, marking carefully where I laid it.

I went out once, at least, every day with my gun, as well to divert myself as to see if I could kill anything fit for food. I also wanted to acquaint myself with what the island produced. The first time I went out, I discovered there were goats on the island, but they were so shy and swift that it was the hardest thing in the world to get close. If they were high on the rocks and saw me in the valleys, they would run away in a terrible fright. If they were feeding in the valleys and I was upon the rocks, they took no notice of me. From this I concluded that they did not readily see objects above them. So I always climbed the rocks first to get above them, and then had frequently a fair mark.

The first shot I made among these creatures I killed a she-goat, which was nursing a little kid, which grieved me heartily. When the goat fell, the kid stood stock still by her. I came and placed the goat on my shoulder, and when I carried her away, the kid followed me all the way to my enclosure. I laid down the she-goat, took the kid in my arms, and carried it into my fortress. I was hoping to raise it up tame, but it would not eat, so I was forced to kill it and eat it myself. These two supplied me with meat a great while, for I ate sparingly and saved my provisions, my bread especially, as much as I could.

I was hundreds of leagues out of the ordinary trade routes, and so I had good reason to expect that I would die in this desolate place and in this desolate manner. The tears would run plentifully down my face when I thought about how I could hardly be thankful for such a life.

But one day, walking with my gun in my hand by the seaside, my reason said, "Well, you are in a desolate condition, it is true. But remember, did not eleven of you come into the boat? Where are the other ten? Why were they not saved, and you lost? Why were you singled out? Is it better to be here, or there?" All evils should be weighed with the good that is in them and contrasted with the worse alternatives.

Then it occurred to me again how well supplied I was and what my situation would be if the ship had not floated from the place where she first struck and been driven so near to the shore that I had time to get all these things out of her. What would have been my case, had I been left in the condition in which I first came on shore, without the essentials for life? "What would I have done without a gun," I said aloud, "without ammunition, without any tools to make anything or to work with, without clothes, bedding, a tent, or any manner of covering?" I had all these in sufficient quantity, and was in a fair way to provide for myself when my ammunition was gone. I was able to see how I could carry on without any want as long as I lived. For I considered from the beginning how I would provide for the accidents that might happen and for the time that was to come, not only after my ammunition was gone but even after my health or strength should fail.

Having set the scene, I will now describe in order, from its beginning, my life in this solitary place. It was, by my account, the 30th of September when I first set foot upon this horrid island, which, I reckoned by observation, to be in the latitude of 9 degrees 22 minutes north of the equator.

7

GETTING ORGANIZED

AFTER I HAD BEEN THERE about ten or twelve days, it came into my head that I would lose track of time, and would even confuse Sabbath days with working days. To prevent this, I carved a sign on a large post, in capital letters, and making it into a large cross, I set it on the shore where I first landed: "I came on shore here on the 30th of September 1659." On the sides of this square post I cut every day a notch with my knife, and every seventh notch was twice as long as the rest, and every first day of the month twice as long again. Thus I kept my own calendar.

Among the many things I brought out of the ship which I didn't mention were pens, ink, and paper, several packages in the captain's, mate's, gunner's, and carpenter's keeping, three or four compasses, some mathematical instruments, charts, and books of navigation. Also I found three good English Bibles, some Portuguese books (among them two or three prayer books), and several other books. And I must not forget, that we had in the ship a dog and two cats. I carried both cats to shore, and the dog jumped out of the ship and swam to shore the day after my first visit to the ship, and was a trusty servant to me for many years. He was good company, except that he could not talk with me. As I observed before, I found pen, ink, and paper, and I used them carefully. While my ink lasted, I kept accurate accounts, but after it was gone, I could not, for I could not make any ink by any means that I could devise.

Among the things I lacked besides ink were a spade, pick-axe, and shovel, and needles, pins, and thread. This lack of tools made work very slow, and it was almost a year before I had entirely finished my little fortress. But why should I have been in a hurry, seeing I had plenty of time? I had nothing else to do except exploring the island to seek food, which I did nearly every day.

I now began to consider seriously my condition and the circumstance I was reduced to. I drew up the state of my affairs in writing, not so much to leave them for my survivors as to comfort myself. I stated in two columns the comforts I enjoyed against the miseries I suffered:

EVIL

1. I am on a horrible, desolate island, without any hope of rescue.
2. I am singled out and separated from all the world to be miserable.
3. I am separated from mankind, banished from human society.
4. I have hardly any clothes to wear.
5. I am without defense from attack of man or animal.
6. I have no one to speak to or to help me.

GOOD

1. But I am alive and not drowned, as all my companions were.
2. But I am singled out, too, from all the ship's crew to be spared from death, and He that miraculously saved me from death can deliver me from this condition.
3. But I am not starving in a barren place with no sustenance.
4. But I am in a hot climate, and if I had more clothes I would hardly wear them.
5. But I see no wild animals on this island to attack me, as I saw on the coast of Africa. What if I had been shipwrecked there?

6. But God wonderfully sent the ship near enough to shore that I got out things enabling me to help myself.

Upon the whole, there is hardly any condition in the world as miserable as mine, yet there is something positive to be thankful for in it. We may always find something to set in the "good" side of the account.

Having now brought my mind to accept my circumstances, I began to apply myself to improve my way of living.

I have already described my home, which was a tent next to a rock, surrounded by a strong fence of posts and cables. I might now call it a wall, for I raised a kind of wall against it of earth and roots, about two feet thick on the outside. After about a year and a half I raised rafters from it leading to the rock and covered it with boughs of trees and any thing else I could find to keep out the rain, which at some times of the year was very violent.

At first my fortress was a confused heap of my possessions in no order, so they took up all my space; I had no room to turn around. So I set myself to enlarge my cave farther into the earth, which consisted of loose sandy rock that yielded easily to my digging. When I found I was safe from beasts of prey, I made a tunnel behind the rock, and at the end made a door on the outside of my fort. This gave me not only a back way to my tent and to my storehouse, but gave me more room to stow my goods.

And now I began to apply myself to make those things I most wanted, particularly a chair and a table, for without these I was not able to enjoy the few comforts I had in the world. I could not write or eat with much pleasure without a table.

I had never handled a tool in my life, and yet in time, by labor, application, and invention, I found I could have made anything, especially if I had tools. However, I made many things even without tools, and some with no more tools than an adze and a hatchet. If I wanted a board, I had no other way but to cut down a tree and hew it flat on either side with my axe, till I had made it thin as a plank, and then dub it smooth with my adze. By this method I could make but one board out of a whole tree, but my time or labor was worth little, and were as well employed one way as another.

I made my table and chair out of the short pieces of boards that I brought on my raft from the ship. But when I had made boards from trees, I made large shelves all along one side of my cave, to lay all my tools, nails, and iron-work so that I might get at them easily. I knocked hooks into the wall of the rock to hang my guns and anything else that would hang up. I had everything so ready at hand that it was a great pleasure to see all my goods in such order, and especially to find my collection so great.

And now I began to keep a journal. At first I was in too much hurry and too disturbed in my mind, and my journal would have been full of many dull things. I probably would have said:

Sept. 30—After I got to shore and had escaped drowning, instead of being thankful to God for my deliverance, having first vomited with the great quantity of salt water I had swallowed, I ran about the shore, wringing my hands and beating my head and face, crying out at my misery, until, tired and faint, I was forced to lie down on the ground to rest. But I didn't dare sleep, for fear of being devoured.

Some days after this, after I had been on board the ship and got everything I could out of her, I could not resist climbing to the top of a little mountain and looking out to sea in hopes of seeing a ship. I then fancied I spied a sail a long ways off, encouraged myself with the hope of rescue, and then, after looking steadily till I was almost blind, lost sight of it altogether, and sat down and wept like a child, thus increasing my misery by my folly.

But having gotten over these things somewhat, and having settled my household stuff and living area, I made me a table and a chair and began to keep my journal. I will here record what I wrote (though in it will be told all these particulars over again) as long as it lasted, for, having no more ink, I was forced to quit.

46

8
DIARY OF A CASTAWAY

SEPTEMBER 30, 1659 —I, poor, miserable Robinson Crusoe, being shipwrecked during a dreadful storm, came on shore on this dismal, unfortunate island, which I call the Island of Despair—all the rest of the ship's company being drowned, and myself almost dead.

All the rest of that day I spent considering the dismal circumstances I was brought to: I had neither food, house, clothes, weapon, nor place to flee to. In my despair I saw nothing but death before me, either that I would be devoured by wild animals, murdered by savages, or starved to death. As night approached, I slept in a tree for fear of wild animals, but slept soundly, though it rained all night.

Oct. 1—In the morning I saw, to my great surprise, the ship had floated with the high tide and was driven on shore much nearer the island. I hoped, if the wind died down, to get on board and acquire some food and necessities for my relief. Yet, on the other hand, it renewed my grief at the loss of my comrades. If we had all stayed on board, we might have saved the ship, or at least they would not have been drowned. Had the men been saved, we might have built us a boat out of the ruins of the ship to carry us to some other part of the world. I spent a great part of this day in troubling myself with these things, but seeing the ship almost dry, I finally swam out to her and climbed on board. This day also it continued raining, though with no wind at all.

Oct. 1 to 24—I spent all these days entirely in making several trips to get all I could out of the ship. I brought many items on shore, every rising tide, upon rafts. Much rain also in these days; it seems this was the rainy season.

Oct. 20—I overturned my raft and all the goods I had on it. But since I was in shoal water, and the things were mostly heavy, I recovered many of them when the tide was out.

Oct. 25—It rained all night and all day, with some gusts of wind. During this time the ship broke in pieces, the wind blowing a little harder than before, and was seen no more, except the wreck of her, and that only at low water. I spent this day in covering and securing the goods I had saved, that the rain might not spoil them.

Oct. 26—I walked about the shore almost all day to find a place to live, greatly concerned to protect myself from an attack at night, either from wild animals or men. Toward night I decided upon a place by a rock, and marked out a semicircle for my camp.

Oct. 26 to 30—I worked hard in carrying all my goods to my new habitation, though part of the time it rained extremely hard.

Oct. 31—In the morning, I went out into the island with my gun to find some food and explore the country. I killed a she-goat, and her kid followed me home, which I afterwards killed also because it would not eat.

Nov. 1—I set up my tent by a rock and lay there the first night, with stakes driven in to swing my hammock upon.

Nov. 2—I set up all my chests and boards and the pieces of timber which made my rafts, and with them formed a fence.

Nov. 3—I went out with my gun and killed two duck-like birds, which were very good food. In the afternoon went to work to make me a table.

Nov. 4—This morning I began to organize my times of work, of going out with my gun, of sleep, and of diversion. Every morning I walked out with my gun for two or three hours, if it did not rain. I then worked till about eleven o'clock, ate, and from twelve to two I lay down to sleep, the weather being excessively hot. In the evening I worked again. The working part of this day and of the next were wholly employed in making my table, for I was yet a poor workman, though time and necessity soon made me skillful.

Nov. 5 —I went out with my gun and my dog and killed a wild cat. Her skin was soft but her meat was good for nothing. Every animal I killed, I took off the skins and preserved them. Coming back by the shore, I saw many sorts of seabirds and two or three seals which, while I was staring, hardly knowing what they were, got into the sea and escaped me for that time.

Nov. 6 —After my morning walk I went to work with my table again and finished it, though not to my liking. But before long I learned to fix it.

Nov. 7 —Now it began to be settled, fair weather. From the 7th to the 12th (except for the 11th, which was Sunday) I worked to make me a chair, and brought it to a tolerable shape, though I wasn't satisfied with it. Even in the making, I pulled it to pieces several times. I soon neglected to keep Sundays for, forgetting to mark them on my post, I forgot which was which.

Nov. 13 —Today it rained, which refreshed me greatly and cooled the earth, but it was accompanied by terrible thunder and lightning. As soon as it was over, I resolved to separate my stock of powder into as many little parcels as possible, that it might not be detonated.

Nov. 14, 15, 16 —These three days I spent making little square chests or boxes, which might hold about a pound or two of powder. I stowed them in places as far from one another as possible. On one of these three days I killed a large bird that was good to eat, but I don't know what to call it.

Nov. 17 —Today I began to dig behind my tent into the rock. I needed three things for this work: a pick-axe, a shovel, and a wheelbarrow, so I began to consider how to make some tools. As for a pick-axe, I made use of iron crowbars, which were proper enough, though heavy. A shovel or spade was so absolutely necessary that I could do nothing well without it, but what kind of one to make, I knew not.

Nov. 18 —The next day, in searching the woods, I found a tree like the Brazilian "iron tree," with extremely hard wood. From this, with great labor, and almost spoiling my axe, I cut a heavy piece and brought it home.

Despite the hardness of the wood, I gradually made it into the form of a shovel, the handle exactly shaped like ours in England. It served well enough for my uses, but never was a shovel made in that way or so long in the making.

As to a wheelbarrow, I figured I could make all but the wheel, but I had no notion of how to go about it. Besides, I had no possible way to make the iron socket for the axle of the wheel to run in, so I gave up. To carry away the earth I dug out of the cave, I made the kind of tray used to carry mortar for bricklayers.

This was not as difficult to make as the shovel, and yet this and the shovel took up no less than four full days, except for my morning walk with my gun.

Nov. 23 —When the tools were finished, I spent eighteen days widening and deepening my cave, so that it would hold my possessions.

Note —Sometimes in the wet season of the year it rained so hard that I could not keep myself dry in my tent, which caused me afterwards to cover all my place with long poles, like rafters leaning against the rock, loaded with flags and large leaves of trees, like a thatched roof.

Dec. 10 —I began to think my cave was finished, when suddenly part of the roof and side fell in. If I had been under it, I would never have needed a grave-digger. After this disaster I had the loose earth to carry out and, more important, I had the ceiling to prop up.

Dec. 11—Today I went to work and got two posts up, with two pieces of boards over each post. In about a week more I had the roof safe, and the posts served as partitions.

Dec. 17—From this day to the twentieth I placed shelves, and hammered nails on the posts to hang everything up that could be hung up. Now I began to get things into order.

Dec. 20—I carried everything into the cave and began to furnish my house, though I began to run out of boards. I also made another table.

Dec. 24—Much rain all night and all day; no stirring out.

Dec. 25—Rain all day.

Dec. 26—No rain, and the earth much cooler than before.

Dec. 27—Killed a young goat and lamed another, so that I caught it and led it home on a string. I bound and splinted its leg, which was broken. By my nursing it so long it grew tame and fed on the grass at my door, and would not go away. This was the first time I entertained the thought of breeding some tame creatures, that I might have food when my powder and shot was all spent.

Dec. 28, 29, 30—Great heat and no breeze, so that there was no stirring abroad, except in the evening, for food. This time I spent in putting all my things in order within doors.

Jan. 1—Very hot still, but I went out early and late with my gun, and lay still in the middle of the day. This evening, going farther into the valleys toward the center of the island, I found there were plenty of goats. I decided to bring my dog to try to hunt them down.

Jan. 2—I went out with my dog and set him upon the goats, but they all faced about upon him. He knew his danger too well, for he would not go near them.

Jan. 3—I began my fence or wall, which I resolved to make thick and strong. Note: I purposely omit what was said in the journal. It is sufficient to observe that I worked from the 3rd of January to the 14th of April finishing and perfecting this wall, though it was only about twenty-four yards long, being a half circle from one place in the rock to another, with the door of the cave in the center behind it.

All this time I worked hard, the rains hindering me for days and sometimes weeks. But I thought I would not be safe till this wall was finished.

When the wall was finished and the outside double-fenced with a turf-wall raised up close to it, I figured that if any people were to come on shore there, they would not see my home. It was good that I did, as I will describe later.

During this time, I made my rounds in the woods for game every day, when the rain allowed it, and made frequent discoveries. I found a kind of wild pigeon, which nested in the holes of the rocks. Taking some young ones, I endeavored to breed them up tame, and did so. But when they grew older they flew away, perhaps because I had nothing to feed them. However, I frequently found their nests and took their young, which were good meat.

I was at a great loss for candles, so that as soon as it was dark, generally by seven o'clock, I was obliged to go to bed. I remembered the lump of beeswax with which I made candles in my African adventure, but I had none of that now. So when I killed a goat I saved the melted fat, and with a little dish made of clay, which I baked in the sun, I made an oil lamp, adding a wick of shredded rope.

It happened that, searching through my things, I found a little bag that had been filled with grain for feeding the poultry on an earlier voyage. The grain was all devoured by rats, and I saw nothing in the bag but husks and dust. Wanting the bag for some other use, I shook the husks of corn out next to my fort before the great rains. About a month or so later, I saw some few stalks of something green shooting out of the ground, which I fancied might be some plant I had not seen. But I was perfectly astonished when, after a little longer time, I saw about ten or twelve ears come out, which were perfect green English barley.

It is impossible to express my astonishment and confusion on this occasion. I had few thoughts of religion in my head and had taken everything that happened to me as chance—or, as we rightly say, what pleases God—without inquiring into the place of Providence in these things, or His order in governing events in the world. But after I saw barley grow there, it startled me, and I began to wonder if God had miraculously caused this grain to grow for my sustenance in that miserable place.

This touched me and brought tears to my eyes, that such a wonder should happen upon my account. Stranger yet, some other straggling stalks came up, which proved to be stalks of rice, which I knew because I had seen it grow in Africa when I was ashore there.

I went all over that part of the island, peering under every rock to find more grain, but I could not find any. At last it occurred to me that I had shaken a bag of chickenfeed out in that place, and then the wonder began to cease. I confess my thankfulness to God began to fade upon discovering that the grain was natural. But I ought to have been as thankful for such an unexpected gift as if it had been miraculous, for it was as much God's will that ten or twelve seeds of grain should remain (when rats had destroyed all the rest) as if it had been dropped from heaven, and that I should throw it out in the shade of a high rock, where it sprang up immediately. If I had thrown it anywhere else, it would have been scorched by the sun.

I carefully saved the ripe ears of this grain, you may be sure, about the end of June. Storing every kernel, I resolved to plant them, hoping in time to have enough to make bread. But it was not till the fourth year that I could allow myself the least of this grain to eat, for I lost all that I sowed the first season—I had sown it just before the dry season, so that it did not come up at all, at least not as it should have done.

Besides the barley, there were twenty or thirty stalks of rice, which I preserved with the same care. I found ways to cook it without baking, though I baked it also. But I return now to my journal.

I worked extremely hard for three or four months to get my wall done. On the 14th of April I closed it up, planning to enter it over the wall by a ladder, so there would be no evidence of a door on the outside.

April 16—I finished the ladder, so I went up with the ladder to the top, pulled it up after me, and let it down on the inside. Within I had ample room, and nothing could enter without first climbing my wall.

The very next day after the wall was finished, I almost was killed. As I was busy in the entrance to my cave, the earth suddenly came crumbling down from the roof of my cave, and two of the posts I had set up in the cave cracked in a frightful manner. I was heartily scared, thinking that the top of my cave was falling in as some of it had done before. Fearing I would be buried in it, I ran to my ladder and climbed over my wall for fear that pieces of the hill might roll down upon me. I no sooner stepped onto the firm ground than I plainly saw it was a terrible earthquake. The ground I stood on shook three times about eight minutes apart—three shocks that would have overturned the strongest building on earth. A great piece of rock fell into the sea with such a terrible noise, such as I never heard in all my life. The very sea was moving violently, and I believe the shocks were stronger under the water than on the island.

I was like one dead or stupefied. The motion of the earth made my stomach sick, as though I were seasick. But the noise of the falling of the rock roused me and filled me with horror. I thought of the hill falling on my tent and burying everything at once, and my soul sank within me.

All this while I had not the least serious religious thought, nothing but the common, "Lord, have mercy upon me!" and when it was over, that went away too.

The air was overcast, as if it would rain, and soon after the wind rose. In less than half an hour it blew a most dreadful hurricane. The sea was covered over with foam and froth, the shore was covered with water, the trees were torn up by the roots. After about five hours it was stark calm again and began to rain very hard. I went in and sat in my tent. But the rain was so violent that my tent was almost beaten down, and I was forced to go into my cave, though afraid and uneasy for fear it would fall on my head.

This violent rain forced me to cut a drain hole through my new wall to let the water out. It continued raining all that night and most of the next day, so that I could not go out. But my mind being more composed, I began to think of what I should do, concluding that if the island was subject to these earthquakes, I must consider building a little hut in an open place. If I stayed where I was, I would certainly, one time or other, be buried alive.

I decided to remove my tent from the place where it stood, which was just under the hanging precipice of the hill. I spent the two next days, the 19th and 20th of April, in planning where and how to remove my tent.

The fear of being swallowed alive made me unable to sleep well, and yet the fear of lying outside without any fence was almost as bad. When I looked about and saw how everything was put in order, how pleasantly concealed I was, and how safe from danger, I was unwilling to move.

April 22—I had three large axes and an abundance of hatchets, but with much chopping knotty hard wood, they were full of notches and dull. Though I had a grindstone, I could not turn it and grind my tools too. This cost me as much thought as a judge would have bestowed upon the life and death of a man. In time I invented a wheel with a string, to turn it with my foot, so that I would have both hands free. This machine cost me a full week's work to bring it to perfection.

April 28, 29—These two days I spent grinding my tools.

April 30—Low on bread, I limited myself to one biscuit a day, which made my heart heavy.

9
A TURNING POINT

MAY 1 —In the morning, looking seaward at low tide, I saw something on shore that looked like a barrel. Near it were two or three pieces of the wreck of the ship, which had been driven on shore by the hurricane. The wreck itself seemed to lie higher out of the water than before. I soon found the barrel was full of gunpowder, but it had taken in water and the powder was caked as hard as stone.

When I came down to the ship I found that the forecastle, which before was buried in sand, was pushed up at least six feet. The stern, which had been broken to pieces, was now tossed up on one side, and the sand was thrown so high on one side of the stern that I could now walk right up to her when the tide was out. I soon concluded it must have been done by the earthquake. Since the ship was more broken open than formerly, there were many things the sea had loosened that the winds and water rolled gradually to the land.

All the inside of the ship was choked with sand. However, I resolved to pull everything to pieces that I could, because everything I could get from her would be of some use or other.

May 3 —I began with my saw, and cut a piece of a beam through, which I thought held some of the upper part or quarter-deck together. When I had cut it through, I cleared away the sand as well as I could, but I had to quit when the tide came in.

May 4—I went fishing but caught nothing that I dared to eat. Just as I was about to quit, I caught a young dolphin. I had made a long line of some rope-yarn, but I had no hooks. Yet I frequently caught as much fish as I cared to eat, which I dried in the sun first.

May 5 —Worked on the wreck, cut another beam in two, and brought three great fir-planks from the decks, which I tied together and floated to shore when the tide came in.

May 6—Worked on the wreck, got several iron bolts out of her, and other pieces of ironwork. Got so tired I felt like giving up.

May 7 —Found the weight of the wreck had broken it down, the beams being cut. Several pieces of the ship seemed to lie loose, and I could see into the hold, but it was almost full of water and sand.

Used an iron crowbar to wrench up the deck, which lay now clear of the water and sand. I wrenched open two planks, and floated them to shore. I left the crowbar in the wreck for the next day.

May 9 —With the crowbar made way into the body of the wreck, and felt several casks and loosened them with the crow, but could not break them open. I felt the roll of sheet lead, but it was too heavy to lift.

May 10 through 14 —Went every day to the wreck, and got a great deal of timber, boards, and much iron.

May 15 —I carried two hatchets to try to cut a piece off the roll of lead, by driving one hatchet with the other. But the lead lay about a foot and a half under the water, and I could not make a dent in it.

May 16 —I stayed so long in the woods to get pigeons for food that the tide prevented me from going to the wreck.

May 17—I saw some pieces of the wreck blown on shore, nearly two miles from me, but resolved to see what they were. I found it was a piece of the head, but too heavy for me to bring away.

May 24 —Every day I worked on the wreck, and with hard labor I loosened some things so much with the crowbar that at the first windy high tide, several casks floated out and two of the seamen's chests.

But nothing came to land that day but pieces of timber and a hogshead which had some Brazil pork in it, which salt water and sand had spoiled.

I continued this work every day to the 15th of June, except the time necessary to get food—which I always did at high tide so that I might be ready when it was out. By this time I had timber, plank, and iron-work enough to have built a good boat, if I had known how. I eventually got almost a hundred pounds of sheet lead.

June 16—Going down to the seaside, I found a large turtle, the first I had seen. If I had happened to be on the other side of the island, I might have had hundreds of them every day, as I found afterwards, but perhaps they would have cost me too much.

June 17—I spent the day cooking the turtle. I found inside her sixty eggs, and her meat was the best I had ever tasted in my life, having had no meat except goats and birds since I landed in this horrid place.

June 18—Rained all day, and I stayed within. The rain felt cold and I was chilled, which I knew was not usual in that latitude.

June 19—Very ill, and shivering, as if the weather had been cold.

June 20—No rest all night. Violent pains in my head, and feverish.

June 21—Very ill, frightened almost to death to be so sick, and no help. Prayed to God for the first time since the storm near Hull, but scarce knew what I said, or why.

June 22—A little better, but dreadful fear.

June 23—Very bad again; cold and shivering, and then a violent headache.

June 24—Much better.

June 25—Chills and fever with shaking for seven hours, with a sweat.

June 26—Better. Having no food, I took my gun, but found myself very weak. However, I killed a she-goat, and with much difficulty got it home, broiled some of it, and ate. I would have stewed it and made some broth, but had no pot.

June 27—Shaking chills and fever again so violent that I lay in bed all day, and neither ate nor drank. I was ready to die from thirst, but so weak I couldn't stand up or get any water. I lay and cried, "Lord, look upon me! Lord, pity me! Lord, have mercy upon me!" I suppose I did nothing else for two or three hours, until I fell asleep, and did not wake till far in the night. When I awoke, I felt rested but weak and extremely thirsty. However, as I had no water in my fortress, I was forced to wait till morning, and went to sleep again. In this second sleep I had this terrible dream.

I dreamt that I was sitting on the ground outside my wall, where I sat when the storm blew after the earthquake, and that I saw a man descend from the great black cloud, in a bright flame of fire. He was as bright as a flame, so that I could barely look toward him. His face was impossible for words to describe. When he stepped upon the ground, I thought the earth trembled, just as it had in the earthquake, and all the air looked as if it were filled with flashes of fire.

He moved toward me, with a long spear in his hand to kill me, and when he came to a hill, he spoke to me in a voice so terrible that it is impossible to describe. All that I understood was this: "Seeing all these things have not brought you to repentance, now you shall die." At those words I thought he lifted up the spear to kill me.

No one who reads this account will expect me to describe the horrors of my soul at this terrible vision, nor is it possible to describe how I felt when I awakened and found it had been a dream.

What I had learned from the good instruction of my father had been worn out by eight years of seafaring wickedness and a constant association with men like myself. I do not remember that I had, in all that time, one thought that so much as tended to look upwards toward God, or inwards to consider my ways. A certain stupidity of soul, without desire for good or awareness of evil, had entirely overwhelmed me. I was all that the most hardened sailors are thought to be, not having the least sense, either of the fear of God in danger or of thankfulness to God in safety.

Through all the various miseries I had experienced to this day, I never had so much as one thought of it being the hand of God, or that it was a just punishment for my rebellious behavior against my father, or for the general course of my wicked life. When I was on the desert shores of Africa, I had no thought of what would become of me or one wish that God would direct me where I should go or keep me from the dangers which surrounded me. I was led by animal instinct and by the dictates of common sense only—and indeed hardly that.

When I was saved at sea by the kind Portuguese captain, I had no thankfulness in my thoughts. When again I was shipwrecked and in danger of drowning on this island, I had no remorse and didn't see it as a judgment. I told myself often that I was born to be unfortunate and miserable.

It is true, when I first got on shore here and found all my ship's crew drowned and myself spared, I was surprised with a kind of ecstasy that, had the grace of God assisted, might have become true thankfulness. But it ended where it began, in my being glad I was alive, without the least reflection upon the hand which had preserved me. It was the same sort of joy seamen generally have after they get safely ashore from a shipwreck, joy they drown in the next bowl of punch and forget almost as soon as it is over.

Even when I became aware of my condition, how I was cast on this dreadful place, out of the reach of human kind, with no hope of rescue—as soon as I saw that I would not starve to death, the thought of this as a judgment from heaven seldom entered my head.

The growing of the grain began to affect me with seriousness as long as I thought it was something miraculous, but as soon as that thought was removed, it wore off.

Even with the earthquake (though nothing could be more terrible), no sooner was the first fright over but the impression it had made wore off also. I had no more sense of God or His judgments than if I had been in the most prosperous condition of life.

But now, when I began to be sick, with a leisurely view of the miseries of death, when my spirits began to sink under the violence of the fever, conscience, that had slept so long, began to awake, and I began to rebuke myself over my past life.

I called out to God, though I cannot say my words expressed desires or hopes; it was the voice of fright and distress. My thoughts were confused, and the horror of dying in such a miserable condition made me dizzy with fear. I hardly knew what my tongue said. It was exclamations such as, "Lord! what a miserable creature I am! If I get too sick, I shall certainly die for lack of help, and what will become of me?" Then I burst out weeping and could say no more for a long time.

Now the good advice of my father came to my mind, along with his prediction, which I mentioned at the beginning of this story, that if I did take this foolish step, I would have leisure later on to reflect upon rejecting his advice when there might be no one to help me. "Now," I said aloud, "my dear father's words are come to pass. God's justice has overtaken me, and I have none to help or hear me. I rejected Providence, which had mercifully put me in a place where I might have been happy. But I would neither see it myself or learn the blessing of it from my parents. I left them to mourn over my folly, and now I am left to mourn over it. I refused their help and assistance, who would have made everything easy for me. Now I have no assistance, no help, no comfort, no advice." Then I cried out, "Lord, be my help, for I am in great distress."

This was the first prayer I had made for many years. But now I return to my journal.

10

FINDING COMFORT

JUNE 28 —I awoke without a fever and got up, because now was my chance to get something to help me when the fever returned the next day. The first thing I did was to fill a large bottle with water and set it on my table, in reach of my bed. Then I got a piece of goat's meat and broiled it on the coals, but could eat very little. I walked about, but was weak and heavy-hearted, dreading the return of my fever the next day. At night I made my supper of three of the turtle's eggs, which I roasted in the ashes. This was the first bit of food I had ever asked God's blessing on, as far as I could remember, in my whole life.

After I had eaten, I tried to walk, but found myself so weak that I could hardly carry the gun (for I never went out without that). So I sat on the ground, looking out upon the calm, smooth sea. As I sat there, thoughts such as these occurred to me.

What is this earth and sea, of which I have seen so much? Where did it come from? And what am I, and all the other creatures, wild and tame, human and animal? Where did we come from? We are all made by some secret Power. And who is that?

Then I realized, God has made it all. Then if God has made all these things, He guides and governs them, for the Power that could make all things must certainly have power to guide and direct them.

If so, nothing can happen without His knowledge or permission.

And if nothing happens without His knowledge, He knows that I am here in this dreadful condition. And if nothing happens without His permission, He has permitted all this to happen to me.

If it is true that God has permitted all this to happen, why has God done this to me? What have I done to deserve it?

My conscience spoke to me like a voice: "Wretch! Do you ask what you have done? Look back upon your dreadful, misspent life and ask yourself what you have not done! Ask why is it that you were not destroyed long ago."

Like someone astonished, I had nothing to say in answer, but rose up thoughtful and sad, walked back to my retreat, and went up over my wall, as if I were going to bed. But I had no inclination to sleep, so I sat in my chair and lighted my lamp, for it was getting dark. As the fear of the fever terrified me, it occurred to my thought that the Brazilians take no medicine but tobacco for almost all illness, and I had some tobacco in one of the chests.

I went, directed by Heaven no doubt, for in this chest I found a cure both for soul and body. I opened the chest and found the tobacco, and as the few books I had saved lay there too, I took out one of the Bibles, which to this time I had not found the time or the inclination to look into. I brought both the Bible and the tobacco with me to the table.

How to use the tobacco I did not know, or even if it was good for my illness. But I tried several experiments with it, including chewing a piece of a leaf and breathing the smoke from some that I burned over a pan of coals, which almost suffocated me.

In the meantime I began to read the Bible, but my head was too disturbed from the tobacco to bear reading right then. I had opened the book at random, and did manage to read the first words I saw, "Call on Me in the day of trouble, and I will deliver, and thou shalt glorify Me."

The words impressed me, though not as much as they did afterwards, for it seemed so impossible in my way of thinking, that I began to ask, Can God Himself deliver me from this place? However, I thought about the words often.

It grew late, so I left my lamp burning in the cave, in case I wanted anything in the night, and went to bed. But before I lay down, I did what I had never done in all my life—I kneeled and prayed to God to fulfill the promise that if I called upon Him in the day of trouble, He would deliver me. After my broken and imperfect prayer was over, I went to bed and fell into a sound sleep. I did not wake up until nearly three o'clock the next afternoon, judging from the sun, but I think it possible that I slept all the next day and night, and till almost three the day after. Otherwise I don't know how I lost a day out of my record of the days of the week, as I discovered years later.

Be that as it may, when I awoke I found myself refreshed, and my spirits lively and cheerful. I was stronger than I was the day before, and my stomach better, for I was hungry, and I had no fever.

On the 30th I went out with my gun, but did not care to travel too far. I killed a seabird or two and brought them home, but did not feel like eating them, so I ate some more of the turtle's eggs, which were very good.

July 3—I got rid of the fever for good, though I did not recover my full strength for some weeks. I thought a lot about the Scripture, "I will deliver thee," and the impossibility of my ever being delivered from the island. But as I was discouraging myself with such thoughts, I realized that I was disregarding the deliverance I had received. I asked myself, "Have I not been delivered, and wonderfully too, from the sickness that was so frightful?" God had delivered me, but I had not glorified Him. If I had not been thankful for that as a deliverance, how could I expect greater deliverance?

This touched my heart very much, and immediately I kneeled and gave God thanks aloud for my recovery from my sickness.

July 4—In the morning I took the Bible, and beginning at the New

In the morning I took the Bible, and beginning at the New Testament, I began to read it.

Testament, I began to read it. I decided to read awhile every morning and every night, not tying myself to any number of chapters.

The message of my dream returned, and the words, "All these things have not brought you to repentance" bothered me. I was earnestly begging God to give me repentance, when it happened that very day that, reading the Scripture, I came to these words, "He is exalted a Prince and a Savior, to give repentance, and to give remission." I threw down the book, and with my heart as well as my hands lifted to heaven, in a kind of ecstasy of joy, I cried out aloud, "Jesus, son of David! Jesus, exalted Prince and Savior, give me repentance!"

This was the first time that I could say, in the true sense of the words, that I prayed in all my life, for now I prayed with a sense of my condition and with encouragement of the Word of God. From this time I began to have hope that God would hear me.

I began to understand the words, "Call on Me, and I will deliver you" in a different sense. Until then I had no notion of anything being called deliverance but my being delivered from my island prison. But now my soul sought nothing from God but deliverance from the load of guilt for my past sins. As for my lonely life, it was nothing in comparison to this. And I add this hint to my readers, that whenever they come to a true sense of things, they will find deliverance from sin a much greater blessing than deliverance from misfortune.

But leaving this part, I return to my journal.

My thoughts being directed by constant Scripture reading and praying to God, I had a great deal of comfort within, which, till now, I knew nothing about. Also, as my health and strength returned, I tried to improve my way of living.

From the 4th of July to the 14th, I spent most of my time walking about with my gun in my hand. It is hard to imagine how weak I was. Though the medical treatment I invented did end my fever, it also harmed me, for I had frequent spasms in my nerves and limbs for some time.

I realized that being outdoors in the rainy season was the most harmful thing to my health, especially in those rains which came with storms and hurricanes of wind.

I had now been on this unhappy island over ten months. All possibility of deliverance seemed to be gone, and I firmly believed that no other human had ever set foot there. Having now completed my home, I wanted to explore more of the island.

It was the 15th of July when I began to survey the island. I went up the creek first. I found, after about two miles, that it was no more than a little brook of running water, and very fresh and good. But this being the dry season, there was hardly any water in some parts of it. On the banks of this brook I found many pleasant meadows, plain, smooth, and covered with grass.

I searched for the cassava root, which Indians make their bread from, but I could find none. I saw aloes, but did not then understand them. I saw several sugar-canes, but wild, and imperfect.

The next day I went up the same way again, and after going farther, I found that the country became more woody. In this part I found different fruits, particularly melons in great abundance and grapes. The grapevines had spread over the trees, and the clusters of grapes were just now in their prime, ripe and rich. This was a surprising discovery, and I was extremely glad. But I was warned by experience not to eat too many of them, remembering that when I was ashore in Barbary, eating wild grapes killed several English slaves there. But I found an excellent use for these grapes—to dry them in the sun and keep them as raisins.

I spent all the night there instead of going home. I got up into a tree, where I slept well. The next morning I proceeded on my journey, traveling nearly four miles due north, with a ridge of hills south and north of me.

At the end of this hike I came to an opening, where the country seemed to descend to the west. A little spring of fresh water, which issued out of the side of the hill, ran due east, and the country appeared so fresh, so green, so flourishing, everything being in a constant flourish of spring, that it looked like a planted garden.

I descended a little into that delicious valley, surveying it with a secret kind of pleasure to think that this was all my own. I was king and lord of all this country, like a lord of a manor in England.

I saw an abundance of cocoa, orange, lemon, and citron trees, but all wild and few bearing fruit, at least not then. However, the green limes I gathered were not only pleasant to eat but wholesome, and I mixed their juice afterwards with water, which made it cool and refreshing.

I had much to gather and carry home. I resolved to lay up a supply of grapes, limes, and lemons for the wet season, which I knew was approaching.

To do this, I gathered a large pile of grapes in one place and a lesser pile in another, and a large mound of limes and lemons in another place. Taking a few of each with me, I traveled toward home and resolved to come again and bring a bag or sack, or what I could make, to carry the rest home.

Having spent three days in this journey, I came home (so I must now call my tent and my cave), but before I got there, the grapes were bruised and spoiled and good for little or nothing. As for the limes, they were good, but I had only a few.

The next day, being the 19th, I went back, having made two small bags to bring home my harvest. But I was surprised when, coming to my heap of grapes, which were so rich and fine when I gathered them, I found them all scattered about, trampled on and devoured. What creatures had done this, I did not know.

I gathered a large quantity of grapes and hung them on outer branches of the trees to dry in the sun, and I carried as many limes and lemons back as I could.

For some time I thought about moving to that fruitful part of the island. But I was now by the seaside, where it was at least possible that something might happen someday. To enclose myself among the hills and woods in the center of the island was to make human contact not only improbable but impossible.

However, I so enjoyed this place that I spent much of my time there for the remaining part of July. I built a little shelter and surrounded it at a distance with a strong fence, being a double hedge as high as I could reach, well staked and filled between with brushwood. I fancied now I had my country house and my seacoast house, and this work took me to the beginning of August.

The rains came on and made me stick close to my first home. Though my second home had a tent also, there was no shelter of a hill there to keep me from storms, nor a cave behind me to retreat into when the rains were extraordinary.

By August 3, the grapes I had hung up were perfectly dried and were excellent good raisins, so I began to take them down from the trees. It was good that I did, for the rains which followed would have spoiled them. They were the best part of my winter food, and I had more than two hundred large bunches of them. No sooner had I taken them all down and carried most of them home to my cave, but it began to rain. From the 14th of August, it rained nearly every day till the middle of October, sometimes so violently, that I could not leave my cave for several days.

During this time, I was much surprised with the increase of my family. I had been concerned about the loss of one of my cats, who had run away or died, and I saw nothing more of her until, to my astonishment, she came home about the end of August with three kittens. This was very strange because the wild cat I had killed with my gun was a quite different kind from our European house cats, yet the young cats were the same kind as their mother. Since both my cats were females, I thought it very strange. But from these three kittens I later came to be so pestered with cats that I was forced to kill some and to drive the rest from my house as much as possible.

From the 14th to the 26th of August it rained continuously, so that I could not go out, being careful not to get wet. In this confinement, I began to be short of food. Venturing out twice, I one day killed a goat, and the last day, which was the 26th, found a large tortoise, which was a treat. This is what I ate each day: A bunch of raisins for my breakfast, a piece of the goat's meat or of the turtle for my dinner, broiled (to my great misfortune, I had no pot to boil or stew anything), and two or three of the turtle's eggs for my supper.

During this time, I worked two or three hours daily at enlarging my cave. I worked one side of it until I gradually came to the outside of the hill, and made a door or way out, beyond my fence or wall. Now I felt less safe, yet I could not perceive that there was any living thing to fear. The biggest creature I had yet seen on the island was a goat.

Sept. 30 —I now came to the unhappy anniversary of my landing. I checked the notches on my post and found I had been on shore three hundred and sixty-five days. I kept this day as a solemn fast, prostrating myself in humility on the ground, confessing my sins to God, acknowledging His righteous judgments upon me, and praying to Him to have mercy on me through Jesus Christ. I did not eat anything for twelve hours, until the sun went down, and I then ate a biscuit-cake and a bunch of grapes and went to bed, finishing the day as I began it.

I had observed no Sabbath days all this time. At first I had no sense of religion and, after some time, stopped making a longer notch than ordinary for the Sabbath day, and so I did not really know what any of the days were. But now that I found I had been there a year, I divided it into weeks and set apart every seventh day for a Sabbath.

A little after this my ink began to run out, and so I contented myself to use less and to write down only the most remarkable events of my life, without continuing a daily record of other things.

The rainy season and the dry season began now to appear regular to me, and I learned by experience to prepare for them. One of the most discouraging experiments that I made concerned the few ears of barley and rice I had carefully saved for planting. I thought it a good time to sow after the rains, so I dug up a piece of ground as well as I could with my wooden spade, and dividing it into two parts, I planted my seed. But I decided not to plant it all at first, so I planted about two-thirds of the seed, leaving about a handful of each.

It was a great comfort to me afterwards that I did so, for not one grain I sowed this time came to anything. Finding that my first seed did not grow, I sought for a moister piece of ground to make another trial in. I dug up a piece of ground near my new shelter and planted the rest of my seed in February. This planting, having the rainy months of March and April to water it, sprouted and grew and yielded a good crop. But since I had planted only a small amount of seed, not daring to plant what little I had left, my whole crop did not amount to more than a gallon of each kind. But by this experiment I knew exactly when the proper season was to plant, and that I could expect two seed-times and two harvests every year.

While this grain was growing, I made a little discovery, which was of use to me afterwards. As soon as the rains were over and the weather began to settle, which was about the month of November, I made a visit to my shelter. Though I had not been there for some months, I found everything just as I left them. The circle or double hedge I had made was not only firm and entire, but the stakes I had cut out of some trees nearby had sprouted and grown long branches. I didn't have a name for the trees. I was surprised, and yet well pleased to see the young trees grow, and I pruned them neatly. It is hard to believe how beautiful they grew in three years. Though the hedge made a circle about twenty-five yards in diameter, the trees soon covered it. It was completely shady, fine to lodge under all the dry season.

I decided to cut some more stakes and make a hedge like this around the wall of my first dwelling, which I did. Placing the trees in a double row, about eight yards from my first fence, they became at first a fine shade for my home, and afterward served for a defense also, as I shall tell later.

11
EXPLORING THE ISLAND

THE YEAR WAS NOT DIVIDED into summer and winter, but into rainy seasons and dry seasons. I stayed inside as much as possible during the wet months.

I kept busy trying to produce things I needed, by hard labor and constant practice. I tried many ways to make myself a basket, but all the twigs I used were so brittle they would do nothing. Fortunately, when I was a boy I used to take delight in standing at a basket maker's in the town where we lived, to see him make his wicker-ware. I was a great observer of how he worked, and being eager to help, as boys usually are, I would sometimes lend a hand. Now I lacked nothing but the materials. Finally it occurred to me that the twigs of that tree from which I cut my stakes that grew might possibly work, and I resolved to try.

The next day I went to my country house, as I called it, and cut some of the smaller twigs. They were all I could desire. The next time I brought a hatchet to cut down a quantity, for there were plenty of them. These I set up to dry, and when they were fit for use, I carried them to my cave. During the dry season I made a great many baskets, both to carry earth and to store things. And though I did not finish them very artistically, they were useful. Afterwards I was careful never to be without them, and as my wicker-ware decayed, I made more. I made strong deep baskets for my future harvest of grain.

Having mastered this difficulty, which took a world of time, I tried to figure out how to supply two other wants. I had no containers to hold anything liquid, except some glass bottles. I didn't even have a pot to boil anything, except for a huge kettle, which I saved out of the ship, and which was too big to make broth or to stew a bit of meat by itself. The second thing I wished for was a pipe, but it was impossible for me to make one. However, I would find a way for that, at last.

I mentioned before that I desired to see the whole island, and had traveled up the brook and built my shelter, from where I had access to the sea on the other side of the island. I now resolved to travel to the seashore on that side. Taking my gun, a hatchet, and my dog, and a larger quantity of powder and shot than usual, with two biscuit-cakes and a great bunch of raisins in my pouch, I began my journey. When I had passed the valley where my shelter stood, I had a view of the sea to the west. It was a clear day, and I could see land, whether an island or a continent I could not tell. But it was far away—by my guess, at least fifteen or twenty leagues off.

I knew it must be part of America, and I concluded that it must be near the Spanish dominions, and perhaps was all inhabited by savages. Had I landed there, I would have been in worse condition than I was now. I have heard about cannibals who murder and devour all the humans that fall into their hands.

With these thoughts, I walked leisurely forward. I found this side of the island much more pleasant than mine, full of sweet meadows adorned with flowers and fine woods.

I saw an abundance of parrots and wanted to catch one, if possible, to tame it and teach it to speak to me. I did eventually catch a young parrot. I knocked it down with a stick and brought it home, but it was some years before I could make him speak. At last I taught him to call me by my name.

I found hares, as I thought them to be, and foxes, but they were different from any I knew of, so I didn't care to eat them. But I had no need to be venturous, for I had plenty of good food, especially goats, pigeons, and turtles which, added to my grapes, furnished my table well. And though my situation was deplorable, I had great cause for thankfulness.

I never traveled on this journey more than two miles or so in a day, but I took so many turns and returns to see what discoveries I could make, that I was weary by night. Then I either slept in a tree or surrounded myself with a row of stakes so no wild animal could come at me without waking me.

As soon as I arrived at the seashore, I was surprised to see that I had settled on the worst side of the island, for here the shore was covered with innumerable turtles. On the other side, I had found only three in a year and a half. Here was also an infinite number of birds of many kinds, many of them good to eat, but I didn't know their names except those called penguins.

I could have shot as many as I pleased, but was saving my powder and shot and was more interested in killing a goat, if I could, which would be better for eating. Though there were many goats here, more than on my side of the island, it was much more difficult to get near them. The country was flat and even, and they saw me much sooner than when I was on the hill.

Though this side of the country was more pleasant than mine, all the while I was here I felt on a journey away from home. I traveled along the shore toward the east for about twelve miles, and then set up a great pole upon the shore for a mark. I decided that the next journey I took should be around the other side of the island, east from my dwelling, till I came to my post again. More about that later.

I took another way to return, thinking I could not miss finding my way home by viewing the country. But I found myself mistaken, for in two or three miles I was in a large valley, surrounded by wooded hills. The weather proved hazy for three or four days while I was in this valley, and not being able to see the sun, I wandered about. At last I was forced to find the seaside, look for my post, and come back the same way I went. The weather was hot, and my gun, ammunition, hatchet, and other things were heavy.

12
A NEW PET

ON THIS JOURNEY my dog surprised a young kid and seized it. I ran and saved it alive from the dog. I had a great mind to bring it home if I could, for I had often wondered whether it would be possible to get a kid or two and raise a breed of tame goats, which might supply me when my powder and shot were all used up.

I made a collar for this little creature, and with some rope which I always carried with me, I led him along, though with some difficulty, till I came to my shelter. There I enclosed him and left him, for I was impatient to get home. I had been gone over a month.

I cannot describe the satisfaction it was to lie in my hammock-bed. My own house, as I called it, felt so comfortable that I resolved I would never go far from it again, while it should be my fate to stay on the island.

I rested for a week, spending most of my time in the weighty affair of making a cage for my parrot. Then I began to think of the poor kid I had penned up in my little circle, and resolved to go and bring it home, or give it some food. I went and found it where I left it, almost starved. Having fed it leaves, I tied it as I did before, to lead it away, but it was so tame now there was no need to have tied it, for it followed me like a dog. As I continually fed it, the creature became so loving, so gentle, and so fond, that it would never leave me.

The rainy season had come, and I kept the 30th of September in the same solemn manner as before—the anniversary of my landing on the island. I had been there two years, with no more prospect of being delivered than the day I arrived. I gave humble and hearty thanks that God had been pleased to show me that it was possible to be more happy in this solitary condition than I would have been in civilization with all the pleasures of the world. I thanked Him that He could fully make up for my isolation by His presence—supporting, comforting, and encouraging me to depend upon His providence here, and hope for His eternal presence hereafter.

I began to feel how much more happy this life I now led was, with all its miserable circumstances, than the abominable life I had led in the past. My very desires were changed, and my pleasures were perfectly new.

Before, as I walked about, the anguish of my soul would sometimes break out suddenly, and my heart would fail within me to think of how I was a prisoner, locked up with the eternal bars and bolts of the ocean, in an uninhabited wilderness. I would weep like a child. Sometimes it would hit me in the middle of my work, and I would sit right down and look at the ground for a solid hour or two. This was worse, for if I could burst out into tears, the grief would exhaust itself sooner.

But now I began to think new thoughts. One morning, being very sad, I opened the Bible to these words, "I will never leave thee, nor forsake thee." Immediately it occurred that these words were for me. "Well, then," I said, "if God does not forsake me, what does it matter though the world forsakes me? If I had all the world, and lost the favor and blessing of God, there would be no comparison in the loss."

From this moment I began to see that it was possible for me to be more happy in this forsaken condition than I was apt to have been in any other situation in the world. With this thought I was going to give thanks to God for bringing me to this place.

I don't know what it was, but something shocked my mind at that thought, and I dared not speak the words. "How can you be such a hypocrite," I said out loud, "to pretend to be thankful for a condition which, however you may try to be contented with, you would rather pray to be delivered from?" So I stopped there; but though I could not say I thanked God for being there, yet I sincerely gave thanks to God for opening my eyes to the former condition of my life, to mourn my wickedness and repent. I never opened the Bible, or closed it, but I blessed God for directing my friend in England to pack it among my goods, and for assisting me to save it out of the wreck of the ship.

Thus I began my third year, and in general I was seldom idle. This is how I spent most of my time: First, my duty to God and reading the Scriptures, three times every day; second, going abroad with my gun for food, which generally took three hours every morning when it did not rain; and third, curing, preserving, and cooking what I had killed or caught. These took up much of the day. In the middle of the day the severity of the heat was too great for activity, so about four hours in the late afternoon was all the time I had to work in.

For lack of tools, lack of help, and lack of skill, everything I did took a long time. It took me forty-two days to make a board for a long shelf I wanted in my cave; two carpenters with saws would have cut six of them out of the same tree in half a day.

It took three days to cut down a large tree, and two more to cut off the boughs and reduce it to a log. With hacking and hewing, I reduced both the sides of it into chips till it began to be light enough to move. Then I turned it and made one side smooth and flat as a board from end to end. Turning that side downward, I cut the other side until the plank was about three inches thick and smooth on both sides. I only give this example to show why it took so much of my time to do so little work.

I was now, in the months of November and December, expecting my crop of barley and rice. The area I had manured or dug up for it was not large, for I had little seed. All of a sudden I found I was in danger of losing it all to enemies of several sorts. First the goats and wild crea tures I called hares tasted its sweetness as soon as it came up, and ate it so close to the ground that it had no time to shoot up into stalks.

I saw no remedy but to enclose it with a fence, which I did with much toil and speed. I got it well fenced in about three weeks. I also shot some of the creatures in the daytime and set my dog to guard it at night, tying him to a stake at the gate, where he would stand and bark all night long. In a short time the enemies forsook the place, and the grain grew strong and well, and began to ripen.

But as the animals ruined the grain in the blade, so the birds were as likely to ruin it in the ear, for I saw my little crop surrounded with birds of all sorts, watching until I should be gone. I immediatcly shot at them, for I always had my gun with me. I had no sooner shot than there rose up a little cloud of birds, which I had not seen at all, from among the grain itself.

I went into it to see what damage was already done, and I found they had spoiled a good deal of it. But since it was still too green for them, the loss was not so great that the remainder wouldn't be a good crop if it could be saved.

I could easily see the thieves sitting in the trees about me, as if they were waiting till I was gone. And it was so, for I was no sooner out of their sight but they dropped down, one by one, into the grain again. Coming up to the fence, I fired again and killed three of them. This was what I wished for, and I treated them as we treat notorious thieves in England—I hanged their dead bodies up in public for a terror to others. It is impossible to imagine how well this worked, for the birds not only left the grain, but they left that part of the island. I never saw a bird near the place as long as my scarecrows hung there.

This I was glad of, you may be sure, and about the end of December I harvested my crop.

All I had to cut it down was one of the broadswords, or cutlasses, which I saved out of the ship. I cut nothing off but the ears, carried them away in a large basket I had made, and rubbed the grain out with my hands. At the end of all my harvesting, I found that out of my gallon of seed I had nearly two bushels of rice, and more than two and a half bushels of barley.

This was a great encouragement to me, and I could see that, in time, it would please God to supply me with bread. And yet here I was perplexed again, for I didn't know how to grind flour, nor how to make bread dough from the flour, nor how to bake it. Nevertheless, I resolved not to eat any of this crop but to save it all for seed for the next season.

It might be truly said that now I worked for my bread. I believe few people have thought much about the strange multitude of little things necessary for making bread.

First, I had no plow to turn up the earth, no spade or shovel to dig it. I had conquered this by making a wooden spade, as I observed before, but this did my work in a wooden manner. And though it cost me many days to make it, yet, for lack of iron, it not only wore out sooner but made my work harder.

How many things I needed to fence the grain, protect it, mow or reap it, carry it home, thrash it, separate the chaff, and store it. Then I would need a mill to grind it, sieves to sift it, yeast and salt to make it into bread, and an oven to bake it. Yet all these things I lacked. I had the next six months to devote myself entirely, by labor and invention, to producing all the things I needed to turn my grain into bread.

13
BAKING BREAD

NOW I HAD enough seed to sow over an acre of ground. It took me a week's work to make a spade, which, when it was done, was but a poor one and very heavy. However, I planted my seed in two large flat pieces of ground near my house, and fenced them in. This took three months because a great part of that time was the wet season, when I could not go out.

I worked indoors when it rained, and I diverted myself with talking to my parrot and teaching him to speak. I quickly taught him his own name, and at last to speak it out pretty loud, "Poll," which was the first word I ever heard spoken on the island by any mouth but my own.

It would make the reader pity me, or laugh at me, to tell how I tried to make clay pots—what odd, misshapen, ugly things they were; how many of them fell in and how many fell out (the clay not being stiff enough to bear its own weight); how many were cracked by the heat of the sun, being set out too hastily; and how many fell to pieces. After having labored hard to find the clay, to dig it, to temper it, to bring it home, and to work it, I could not make more than two large earthen ugly things (I cannot call them jars) in about two months' labor.

However, as the sun baked these two dry and hard, I lifted them gently and set them in two large wicker baskets I had made for them,

I diverted myself with talking to my parrot and teaching him to speak.

so they would not break. Between the pot and the basket there was a little room to spare, and I stuffed it full of straw. Because these two pots would be dry, I thought they would hold my grain and perhaps the flour made from the grain.

I made several smaller pottery things with better success, such as little round pots, flat dishes, and pitchers, and the heat of the sun baked them hard. But I wanted an earthen pot to hold liquids and endure the fire, which none of these could do. It happened after some time, making a large fire for cooking my meat, that when I went to put it out, I found a broken piece of one of my clay pots, burnt as hard as a stone and red as a tile. I said to myself that certainly unbroken pots might be made to burn as hard as stone.

I had no notion of building a kiln, but I placed three large pots and two or three smaller ones in a pile, one upon another, and placed firewood all around it, with a large pile of embers under them. I piled fresh fuel around the outside and on the top, till I saw that the pots were red-hot and did not crack at all. I let them stay in that heat about five or six hours, till I found one of them was starting to melt, for the sand which was mixed with the clay melted and would have turned into glass if I had gone on. So I cooled my fire down gradually and watched all night, that I might not let the fire go down too fast. In the morning I had several very good, I will not say handsome, pots, as hard burnt as could be desired, and one of them perfectly glazed by the melting of the sand.

After this experiment, I had no lack of earthenware, but I must admit their shapes were sloppy, as any one may suppose, when I had no way of making them but as children make mud pies.

I could hardly wait till the pots were cold before I set one on the fire again, with some water in it, to boil myself some meat, which it did admirably well. With a piece of goat's meat I made some very good broth, though I lacked oatmeal and several other ingredients to make it as good as I would have liked.

My next concern was to get a stone mortar to grind grain. I spent many days searching for a large stone big enough to cut hollow, and make it fit for a mortar. I could find none at all. The rocks on the island were all of a sandy crumbling stone, which would not bear the weight of a heavy pestle or would add sand to the grain. So, after much lost time in searching for a stone, I gave up and decided to look about for a large block of hard wood, which I found much easier. I rounded it and formed it on the outside with my axe and hatchet, and then, with the help of fire and infinite labor, made a hollow place in it, as the Indians in Brazil make their canoes. After this, I made a heavy pestle of iron-wood. I planned to grind, or rather pound, my next crop of grain into meal, to make my bread.

My next difficulty was to make a sifter to separate the bran and the husk, without which I did not see how I could have any bread. This was most difficult, for I had no fine thin canvas or cotton cloth to sift the meal through. The linen I had was mere rags. I had goat's hair, but no tools or knowledge for making it into cloth. At last I remembered I had, among the seamen's clothes saved out of the ship, some neckcloths of calico or muslin. From pieces of these I made three small sifters that worked for years.

Baking was the next problem. I had no yeast, but I did not concern myself much about it. For an oven, however, I was at a loss. At length I tried an experiment: I made some earthen vessels about two feet in diameter and not more than nine inches deep. These I burned in the fire and set them aside. When I wanted to bake, I made a large fire upon my hearth, which I had paved with some square tiles, of my own making. When the firewood was burned into embers or live coals, I drew them out upon the hearth and let them lie till the hearth was very hot. Then sweeping away all the embers, I set down my loaves, placed the earthen pot over them, and drew the embers around the outside of the pot, to keep in and add to the heat. And thus, as well as in the best oven in the world, I baked my barley-loaves and became, in little time, a pastry-cook in the bargain. I made myself several cakes of the rice and puddings, but I made no pies.

It is no wonder that all these things took up most of the third year of my time here, for I also had my new harvest and animals to manage. I reaped my grain in its season and carried it home as well as I could, and stored it in the ear in my large baskets, till I had time to rub the grain loose with my hands.

And now I wanted to build my barns bigger. I had about twenty bushels of barley, and as much rice or more, so much that I decided to begin to use it freely. My bread from the ship had been gone a great while, and I decided to see how much grain would last me a whole year, and to sow but once a year.

Upon the whole, I found that the forty bushels of barley and rice was much more than I could consume in a year. So I determined to sow just the same amount every year that I sowed the last, in hopes that this would fully provide me with what I needed.

14

GREAT IMPROVEMENTS

MY THOUGHTS returned often to the mainland which I had seen from the other side of the island, and I was not without secret wishes that I were on shore there. From an inhabited country, I might find some means of escape.

But I made no allowance for how I might fall into the hands of savages, perhaps far worse than the lions and tigers of Africa. If I came into their power, I should run a hazard more than a thousand to one of being killed, and perhaps eaten; for I had heard that the people of the Caribbean coasts were cannibals. Suppose they were not cannibals, yet they might kill me, as many Europeans who had fallen into their hands had been. I ought to have considered that, but my head was full of thoughts of getting to the shore.

Now I wished for my boy Xury, and the long-boat which I sailed over a thousand miles along the coast of Africa; but this was in vain. Then I thought I would go and look at our ship's boat, which was blown onto the shore in the storm when I became a castaway. She was turned almost bottom upward, against a high ridge of rough sand.

If I had had helpers to fix her and launch her into the water, the boat would have done well enough, and I might have gone back to the Brazils. But I could no more turn her and set her upright than I could move the island.

I spent three or four weeks trying it. Finding it impossible to heave it up, I fell to digging away the sand, to undermine it and make it fall down, setting pieces of wood to thrust and guide it right in the fall. But when I had done this, I was unable to stir it up again, or to get under it, much less to move it forward toward the water; so I was forced to give up. And yet my desire to venture over to the mainland increased, rather than decreased.

At last I wondered whether it wasn't possible to make myself a canoe such as the natives of those climates make of the trunk of a great tree. This I not only thought possible, but easy, and pleased myself extremely with the idea of making it.

One would think I should have wondered immediately how I should get it into the sea; but my thoughts were so intent upon my voyage over the sea that I never once considered how I should get it off of the land. Yet it would have been easier for me to guide it over forty-five miles of sea than forty-five yards of land.

I went to work upon this boat like the biggest fool ever. Of course the difficulty of launching my boat came often into my head; but I put a stop to my own questions with this foolish answer which I gave myself, "Let's first make it! I'll find some way or other to get it to the water when it's ready."

First I chopped down a cedar tree. I doubt whether Solomon ever had such a tree for the building of the temple of Jerusalem. It was five feet ten inches in diameter at the lower part next the stump, and four feet eleven inches in diameter at the end of twenty-two feet, after which it was smaller, and then parted into branches. It was not without infinite labor that I felled this tree. I was twenty days hacking and hewing at it at the bottom and fourteen more cutting off the branches and limbs and its vast, spreading head which I hacked and hewed through with axe and hatchet. After this, it cost me a month to shape it into something like the bottom of a boat. It cost me nearly three months more to clear the inside and turn it into a boat. This I did by mere mallet and chisel, and by hard labor, till I had a boat big enough to have carried twenty-six men, and consequently big enough to have carried me and all my cargo.

I was extremely delighted with it. Many a weary stroke it had cost, you may be sure. Now there remained nothing but to get it into the water.

But all my efforts to get it into the water failed, though they cost me infinite labor. It lay only about one hundred yards from the creek, but it was uphill towards the creek. I decided to dig and lower the earth, but I could no more stir the canoe than I could the other boat.

Then I measured the distance to the creek, and resolved to cut a canal to bring the water to the canoe, seeing I could not bring the canoe down to the water. Well, I began this work; but when I began to calculate how deep the canal was to be dug, how broad, how much earth to be thrown out, I found that with the number of workers I had, being one, it would take ten or twelve years before I could finish; for the upper end of the canal would have to be at least twenty feet deep. So at length, with great reluctance, I gave up this attempt also.

This grieved me; and now I saw, though too late, the folly of beginning a work before we count the cost and judge correctly our strength.

In the middle of this work I finished my fourth year in this place and kept my anniversary. By a constant study of the Word of God, and with His help, I had gained new understanding. Now I had a different notion of things. I looked upon the world as something remote which I had nothing to do with, no expectation from, and, indeed, no desires about. In a word, I had nothing indeed to do with it. It looked (as it may look to us in the next life) like a place I had lived in long ago.

Here I was removed from all the wickedness of the world. If I pleased, I might call myself king or emperor over the whole country. There were no rivals. I could have raised shiploads of grain, but I had no use for it. I had lots of turtles, but one now and then was all I could put to any use. I had timber enough to have built a fleet of ships. I had grapes enough to have made wine to have loaded that fleet of ships had they been built.

Only what I could use was valuable. If I killed more meat than I could eat, the dog would eat it, or the rats. If I sowed more grain than I could eat, it would spoil. The trees I cut down were lying to rot on the ground; I could only use them for fuel to cook my food.

In other words, I learned that all the good things of this world are no good to us except for our use. The most greedy miser in the world would have been cured had he been in my situation. I had, as I hinted before, a great deal of money, as well gold as silver, about thirty-six pounds sterling. Alas! there the useless stuff lay; and I often thought that I would have given a handful of it for some tobacco-pipes, or for one handmill to grind my grain. Better yet, I would have given it all for six-pennyworth of turnip and carrot seed from England, or for a handful of peas and beans, and a bottle of ink. As it was, I had not the least benefit from it; but there it lay in a drawer, and grew moldy with the damp of the cave in the wet season. If the drawer had been full of diamonds, they would have been of no value to me.

I frequently sat down to my food with thankfulness and admired the hand of God's providence, which had spread my table in the wilderness. I learned to look more upon the bright side of things and less upon the dark side, and to concentrate on what I enjoyed rather than what I lacked. Some people cannot enjoy what God has given them because they are looking at something that He has not given them. All our discontents about what we want spring from the lack of thankfulness for what we have.

Another great help to me was to compare my present condition to how much worse it would have been if God had not wonderfully caused the ship to end up nearer to the shore, so that I could get things for my relief and comfort. Otherwise I would have lacked tools, weapons, and gun-powder.

I spent whole days imagining how I would have acted if I had got nothing out of the ship. I could not have got any food except fish and turtles, and I might have perished first. If I had got any food, I would have had to tear at it with my hands and teeth.

This made me very thankful for my present condition, with all its hardships and misfortunes. I advise other people to consider how much worse their case might be if Providence had not made it easier.

I had another comfort: comparing my present condition with what I deserved. I had lived a dreadful life. I had been well instructed by father and mother; they had tried to teach me respect for God and a sense of duty. Going early into the seafaring life and into seafaring company, my sense of religion was laughed out of me by my companions. I was hardened by frequent danger and scenes of death and by my lack of contact with good influences.

In my escape from Sallee, my being rescued by the Portuguese captain, my flourishing in the Brazils, my receiving cargo from England, and the like, I never had once thought or said the words, "Thank God." In my greatest distress I had never thought to pray to Him or to say, "Lord, have mercy upon me!" I never mentioned the name of God, unless it was to swear.

When I looked about me and considered how God had not only punished me less than I deserved, but had provided for me, this gave me great hope that my repentance was accepted and that God had mercy in store for me.

I worked my mind up to a sincere thankfulness for my condition, seeing that I ought to rejoice for that daily bread which nothing but a crowd of wonders could have brought. I had been fed by a miracle as great as that of ravens feeding Elijah—no, by a long series of miracles.

My life was a life of sorrow in one way, but it was a life of mercy in another. All I needed was to be able to sense God's goodness to me, and His care over me. After I saw this, I was no longer sad.

I had now been here so long that many things I brought on shore for my help were either gone or nearly gone. I had so little ink left that I diluted it with water, more and more, till it was so pale it scarce left any mark on the paper. As long as it lasted, I used it to note the days when any remarkable thing happened to me. If I had been superstitious about days as fatal or fortunate, I might have looked upon certain coincidences with a great deal of curiosity.

On the same day of the year that I left my father and my friends, and ran away to Hull in order to go to sea, the same day later I was captured by the Sallee man-of-war and made a slave.

On the same day of the year that I escaped out of the shipwreck in Yarmouth Roads, that same day years later I made my escape from Sallee in the boat.

On the same day of the year when I was born, the 30th of September, that same day I had my life miraculously saved twenty-six years later when I was cast ashore on this island.

After my ink ran out, so did my bread; I mean the biscuits I saved from the ship. I had allowed myself only one biscuit a day for over a year; and yet I was without any bread for nearly a year before I got any grain of my own.

My clothes began to decay, too, mightily. It was a very great help to me that I had, among all the men's clothes from the ship, almost three dozen shirts. There were also several thick coats, but they were too hot to wear. Though the weather was so hot that there was no need for clothes, yet I could not go naked, though I was all alone.

The reason why I could not go naked was that I could not bear the heat of the sun so well when naked as with some clothes on. With a shirt on, the air itself made some motion, and whistling under that shirt, was cooler than without it. I could never bring myself to go out in the heat of the sun without a cap or hat. The heat of the sun shining directly on my head would give me a headache so that I could not bear it; but if I put on my hat, it would go away.

I began to think about putting the few rags I had, which I called clothes, into some order. I decided to try to make vests out of the large coats; so I set to work tailoring, or rather, botching, for I did a pitiful job on them. However, I managed to make two or three new vests, which I hoped would serve me a great while. As for breeches or trousers, I made a very poor attempt.

I have mentioned that I saved the skins of all the four-footed creatures that I killed, and I had hung them up stretched out with sticks in the sun. Some became dry and hard, but others were very useful. The first thing I made of these was a great cap for my head, with the hair on the outside to repel the rain. This worked so well that I made myself a suit of clothes out of these skins: a vest and knee-length breeches, both very loose, for they were intended to keep me cool rather than warm. I must admit that they were wretchedly made; for if I was a bad carpenter, I was a worse tailor. However, they were very useful. When I was out, if it happened to rain, my vest and cap kept me dry.

After this I spent a great deal of time making an umbrella. I had seen them made in the Brazils, where they are useful in the heat; and I felt the heat even more here, being nearer the equator. It was most useful in the rain as well as the heat. I took a world of pains at it, but after I thought I had found the way, I spoiled two or three. At last I made one that would open and close, and I covered it with skins, When I had no need of it, I could close it and carry it under my arm.

Thus I lived mighty comfortably, resigned to the will of God and throwing myself wholly upon His care. When I missed human conversation, I would ask myself whether conversing with my own thoughts and, if I may say so, with God Himself, was not even better than the best human company in the world.

15
OCEAN DANGER

I CANNOT SAY that for the next five years anything extraordinary happened to me. I lived on just as before. Besides my yearly labor of planting barley and rice, and drying my raisins, and my daily labor of going out with my gun, I had one more labor—to make another canoe, which at last I finished. By digging a canal to it six feet wide, and four feet deep, I got it into the creek, almost half a mile. The first canoe lay where it was, as a memorandum to teach me to be wiser next time.

I was nearly two years making the second canoe, yet I never grudged my labor, in hopes of having a boat to go off to sea at last. But it was too small to venture more than forty miles to the mainland, so I gave up that idea. My next plan was to make a tour round the island. Now that I had a boat, I thought of nothing but sailing around the island.

For this purpose, I made a little mast and a sail out of a piece of the ship's sail which I had saved. Then I made little boxes, at both ends of my boat, to keep provisions and ammunition dry from rain and the spray of the sea, and a long one for my gun.

I fastened my umbrella up like an awning. Thus every now and then I took a little voyage upon the sea, but never went far out from the creek. At last, I put in two dozen of my little loaves of barley bread, an earthen pot full of parched rice, a food I ate a great deal of, a little bottle of rum, half a goat, and powder and shot for killing more, and two large coats—one to lie upon, and the other to cover me at night.

It was the 6th of November, in the sixth year of my reign—or my captivity if you please, that I set out on this voyage, and I found it much longer than I expected. Though the island itself was not very large, on the east side of it I found a great ledge of rocks about two leagues into the sea, some above water, some under it, and beyond that a shoal of sand; so I was obliged to go a great way east out to sea to get past the point.

When first I discovered this problem I dropped the anchor I had made from a piece of a broken grappling which I got out of the ship. Having anchored my boat, I took my gun and went on shore, climbing up a hill which overlooked that point. From the hill I could see a powerful current close to the point which ran to the east; and I saw that when I came into it I might be carried out to sea and not be able to get back to the island again.

I waited there two days for the wind to change. The third day, in the morning, the sea was calm, and I ventured out. But let me be a warning to all rash, ignorant seafarers; for no sooner had I come to the point, not even a boat's length from shore, but I found myself in a current like a rapids. It carried my boat along violently, farther and farther out. There was no wind stirring to help me, and all I could do with my paddles came to nothing. And now I began to give myself up for lost, for I had no prospect before me but of perishing—not by drowning, for the sea was calm enough, but by starving to death. I had indeed found a tortoise on the shore, almost as big as I could lift, and had tossed it into the boat; and I had a great earthen pot of fresh water. But what was all this out in the vast ocean!

Now I looked back upon my desolate island as the most pleasant place in the world, and all the happiness my heart could wish for was back there. I stretched out my hand to it with longing. "O beautiful land!" I said, "I shall never see you again." What I would have given to

100

be on shore. Thus we never know how to value what we enjoy until we lose it. It is impossible to imagine my alarm in being driven from my beloved island (for so it appeared to me now) into the wide ocean. However, I worked hard, and kept my boat as much to the northward as I possibly I could. When about noon, I thought I felt a little breeze of wind in my face, this cheered my heart a little. By this time I was a frightful distance from the island; and I had no compass on board. I should never have known how to steer towards the island if I had once lost sight of it. But the weather continued clear, and I spread my sail.

Just then I saw by sudden clearness of the water that the current was slowing. I found that some ocean rocks caused the current to split apart; and as the main part of it ran southeast, the other returned in an eddy to the northwest.

They who know what it is to have a pardon brought to them when they are on the hangman's ladder, or to be rescued from murderers, may guess how gladly I put my boat into the stream of this eddy and how gladly I spread my sail, running cheerfully before the wind with the eddy under foot.

When I came near the island, I found myself on the northern side, across from where I set out. It still took hours to get to shore, and when I got there, I fell on my knees and gave God thanks for my rescue. I refreshed myself with what I had, brought my boat close to the shore in a little cove that I had spied under some trees, and lay down to sleep, being exhausted by the voyage.

I was now at a great loss which way to get home with my boat. I wouldn't think of attempting it by the way I had come, and what might be at the west side of the island I knew not. So I decided in the morning to make my way westward along the shore, to look for a creek where I might leave my canoe in safety, so as to have her again if I wanted her. In about three miles along the shore, I came to a good inlet which became a very little brook, where I found a convenient harbor for my boat, and where she lay as if she were in a little dock made on purpose for her. After I stowed my boat safely, I went on shore to look about.

I soon found I was near where I had been before when I traveled on foot there. So taking nothing out of my boat but my gun and my umbrella, for it was very hot, I began my hike. This was comfortable enough after the voyage I had been on, and I reached my country house in the evening.

I got over the fence and lay in the shade to rest, for I was very weary, and fell asleep. But imagine, if you can, what a surprise it was when I was waked out of my sleep by a voice calling my name several times, "Robin, Robin Crusoe, poor Robin Crusoe! Where are you, Robin Crusoe? Where are you? Where have you been?"

I was so dead asleep at first, being fatigued from paddling the first part of the day and walking the rest, that I did not wake thoroughly; but I thought I dreamed that somebody spoke to me. As the voice continued to repeat "Robin Crusoe, Robin Crusoe," at last I began to wake more, and was at first dreadfully frightened. But no sooner were my eyes open, than I saw my Poll sitting on top of the fence, and immediately knew that it was he that spoke to me as I had taught him; and he had learned it so perfectly, that he would sit upon my finger, and lay his bill close to my face, and cry, "Poor Robin Crusoe! Where are you? Where have you been?"

However, even though I knew it was the parrot, and that indeed it could be nobody else, it was a good while before I could calm myself. First, I wondered how the creature had got here, and how he had stayed here instead of somewhere else. But I held out my hand and called him by his name, and he came and sat on my thumb as he used to do, and continued saying, "Poor Robin Crusoe" just as if he were overjoyed to see me again; and so I carried him home along with me.

I had now had enough of rambling to sea for some time, and had enough to do for many days to sit still and think about the danger I had been in. I would have been glad to have my boat back on my side of the island; but I didn't know how to get it. The east side of the island made my very heart shrink and my blood run chill just to think of it. As for the west side of the island, I might run the risk of being caught by the same current and carried east past the island, as I had been before of being carried away from it. So with these thoughts, I contented myself to be without any boat, though it had been the product of so many months' labor and of so many more to get it into the sea.

For nearly a year after this I lived a quiet life, feeling happy about everything except the isolation.

During this time I perfected my earthenware pottery by inventing a potter's wheel, which I found infinitely easier and better, because I could make things round and smooth now. But I think I was never more proud than when I made a clay tobacco-pipe. Although it was ugly, it was hard and firm, and would draw the smoke. I was very fond of it, for I always used to smoke. I had found pipes in the ship, but I had forgotten them; and afterwards, when I searched the ship again, I could not find them at all.

As my supply of gunpowder shrank, I began to consider what I must do when I should have no more—that is to say, how I would kill goats then. As I said, I had in my third year on the island caught a young kid and bred her up tame, and I was in hope of getting a he-goat. But I could never find it in my heart to kill her, so she died at last of old age.

16
A DAIRY FARM

IT WAS NOW IN THE ELEVENTH YEAR of my residence, and my ammunition was growing low. I planned to trap some goats, and I particularly wanted a she-goat who would soon give birth to a kid.

I made snares for them, but I had no wire, and I always found the snares broken and my bait devoured. At length I resolved to try a pitfall; so I dug several large pits, in places where I had observed the goats feeding, and over these pits I placed traps, but again the goats stole the bait, for I could see the mark of their feet. I kept changing my traps, until one morning I found in one of them a large old he-goat, and in one of the others three kids, a male and two females.

The old one was so fierce I dared not get near him, so I let him out and he ran away, frightened out of his wits. But I had forgotten then what I learned afterwards, that hunger will tame a lion. If I had let him stay there three or four days without food, and then given him some water and grain, he would have been as tame as one of the kids.

However, I let him go, knowing no better. Then I went to the three kids, and taking them one by one, I tied them together, and with some difficulty brought them all home. I thought that perhaps I could have them near my house like a flock of sheep.

Then it occurred to me that I must keep the tame goats away from the wild goats, or else they would eventually run away. So I needed a fenced area with vegetation for them to eat, water to drink, and shade from the sun.

At first I planned to enclose a large meadow with about two miles of fence. But I did not consider that my goats would be as wild in that large space as if they had the whole island, and with all that room I could never catch them.

When this thought occurred to me I stopped short and decided to enclose a piece of about 150 yards long and 100 yards wide, which would maintain as many goats as I should have for a long time. I spent about three months building the fence, and in the meantime I tethered the three kids nearby, and very often I would take them some barley or rice and feed them out of my hand. After my enclosure was finished and I let them loose, they would follow me up and down, bleating for a handful of grain.

In about a year and half I had a flock of about twelve goats; and in two years more I had forty-three, besides several that I had killed for my food. And after that I enclosed five different pieces of ground to feed them in, with little pens to drive them into, and gates from one area into another.

But this was not all, for now I not only had goat's meat to eat when I pleased, but milk too, a thing which I had not even thought of earlier. So now I set up a dairy, and had sometimes a gallon or two of milk in a day. I, who had never milked a cow, much less a goat, or seen butter or cheese made, after many tries finally learned to make myself both butter and cheese, and never lacked it from that time on.

What a table was spread for me in a wilderness, where at first I saw nothing ahead but perishing from hunger! How like a king I dined, attended by my servants. Poll, my favorite, was the only person permitted to talk to me. My dog, who was now grown very old and crazy, sat always at my right hand; and two cats, one on each side of the table, expecting now and then a bit from my hand, as a mark of special favor. These were not the two cats which I brought on shore, for I had buried both of them near my home with my own hands; but before that one of them had somehow reproduced, and these were the two kittens which I had kept. In this pleasant manner, I lived, short of nothing but company; and of that I would be getting too much in the future.

I had a strange urge to go down to the point of the island, where I once went up the hill to look out. This desire increased every day, and at length I decided to walk there, following the edge of the shore. But if anyone in England had met such a man, it would have frightened him, or made him laugh. I had to smile at the notion of my traveling through Yorkshire in such clothes.

I had a great high shapeless cap, made of a goat's skin, with a flap hanging down behind to keep the sun and rain off my neck.

I had a short jacket of goat's skin coming down to about the middle of my thighs. My breeches were made of the skin of an old he-goat whose hair hung down on either side to the middle of my legs. I had no stockings and shoes, but had made a pair of somethings—I scarce know what to call them—to flap over my legs, and lace on either side.

I had on a broad belt of goat's skin, which I held together with two thongs; and on it hung a little saw and a hatchet, one on one side, one on the other. I had another belt, not so broad, which hung over my shoulder. At the end of it, under my left arm, hung two pouches; in one hung my powder, in the other my shot. At my back I carried my basket, on my shoulder my gun, and over my head a great goatskin umbrella—the most important thing of all, next to my gun. I once let my beard grow till it was about nine inches long; but as I had adequate scissors and razors, I had cut it pretty short, except what grew on my upper lip, which I had trimmed into a huge mustache such as I had seen worn by some Turks.

So I went on my new journey, and was out five or six days. I traveled first along the seashore, directly to the place where I first brought my boat to anchor and climbed the hill. Up there again, I was surprised to see the sea all smooth and quiet, no rippling, no motion, no current, any more there than in other places. I became convinced that the current flowed only at ebb tide, and that the wind caused it to come near or go farther from the shore. Waiting till evening, I went up to the rock again, and I plainly saw that my theory was correct.

This observation convinced me that I had nothing to do but to observe the ebbing and the flowing of the tide, and I might safely bring my boat around the island again. But when I began to think of doing that, I felt too much terror. Instead, I decided that I would make myself another canoe; and so have one for one side of the island, and one for the other.

You are to understand that now I had, as I may call it, two plantations in the island. My first one had the cave, which by this time I had enlarged into several caves. The one which was the driest and largest, and had a door to the outside, was all filled up with the large earthen pots, and with fourteen or fifteen great baskets, which would hold five or six bushels each, where I stored my grain.

By this time my wall of trees had grown so big that there was not the least appearance of any home behind them.

A little farther inland lay my two grainfields. Farther yet, I had my country home. Under the tent there I had made a couch from the skins of the creatures I had killed and other soft things, and a blanket laid on them, from our sea-bedding which I had saved, and a great coat to cover me.

Next to this I had my enclosures for my goats. The living hedge there was strong like a wall, indeed, stronger than any wall. This dairy was a living storehouse of meat, milk, butter, and cheese for me as long as I lived there, even if it were to be forty years.

Here also I had my grapes growing, which I never failed to preserve as raisins, the tastiest part of my diet. And they were very nourishing.

As this home was about half-way between my first home and my boat, I generally stayed all night here on my way to it; for I used to visit my boat to take care of it. Sometimes I went out in it for fun, but scarcely ever more than a stone's throw from shore, I was so fearful of currents or winds or other accidents. But now I come to a new scene in my life.

I saw the print of a man's bare foot on the shore . . .
I stood like one thunderstruck, or as if I had seen a ghost.

110

17
THE FOOTPRINT

ONE DAY AT ABOUT NOON, on my way to my boat, I saw the print of a man's bare foot on the shore, very plain in the sand. I stood like one thunderstruck, or as if I had seen a ghost. I listened, I looked round me, I could hear nothing, nor see anything. I went up to a higher spot, to look farther. I went up and down the shore, but I could see only that one.

I went to it again to make sure; and there was exactly the very print of a foot—toes, heel, and every part of a foot. How it came there I could not in the least imagine. I headed home, terrified, looking behind me at every two or three steps, and fancying every distant stump to be a man.

When I came to my castle, for so I called it after this, I fled into it like one pursued. Whether I went over by the ladder, or went in at the hole in the rock which I called a door, I could not remember the next morning, for never did a frightened hare flee to safety with more terror than I did.

I slept none that night. Sometimes I fancied it must be the devil's footprint, for how should any other thing in human shape come here? But it seemed to me that the devil might have found better ways to terrify me than this of the single print of a foot. Surely he would never have been so stupid as to leave a footprint in a place where it was ten thousand to one whether I should ever see it or not, and in the sand too, where it would soon be erased. All this seemed inconsistent with the notions we usually have of the cleverness of the devil.

I presently reasoned that it must be some more dangerous creature than the devil, some of the savages from the mainland who had wandered out to sea in their canoes, and, either driven by the currents or by contrary winds, had made the island, and had been on shore, but were gone away to sea again.

Then terrible thoughts racked my imagination about their having found my boat, and that they would look for me and devour me; and if it should happen that they could not find me, they would find my enclosure, destroy all my grain, carry away all my tame goats, and I should starve.

Thus my fear banished all my Christian hope. All my former confidence in God, which was founded upon my wonderful experience of His goodness, now vanished. I regretted my confidence that I didn't sow any more grain in one year than just enough to get me to the next season, as if no accident could destroy the crop. So I resolved for the future to have two or three years' corn on hand, so that, whatever might come, I might not perish for lack of food.

How strange life is! Today we love what tomorrow we hate; today we seek what tomorrow we shun; today we desire what tomorrow we fear. My only sorrow was that I had no human company, that I was alone, cut off from mankind. To have seen one of my own species would have seemed to me the greatest blessing that Heaven itself, next to the supreme blessing of salvation, could bestow. Yet now I trembled from fear of seeing a man, and was ready to sink into the ground at the sign of a man's having set his foot in the island!

I decided 'twas my unquestioned duty to resign myself absolutely and entirely to God's will; and, on the other hand, it was my duty also to hope in Him, pray to Him, and quietly to attend to His daily providence.

These thoughts filled my mind many hours, days, weeks, and months. One morning early, lying in my bed, and filled with thoughts about my danger from savages, I was upset; and these words of the Scripture came into my thoughts, "Call upon Me in the day of trouble, and I will deliver, and thou shalt glorify Me."

Upon this, rising cheerfully out of my bed, my heart was not only comforted, but I was guided and encouraged to pray earnestly to God for deliverance. When I had done praying, I took up my Bible, and opening it to read, the first words that presented to me were, "Wait on the Lord, and be of good cheer, and He shall strengthen thy heart; wait, I say, on the Lord." It is impossible to express the comfort this gave me. In answer, I thankfully laid down the book, and was no longer sad, at least not on that occasion.

It came into my thought one day that this foot might be the print of my own foot, when I came on shore from my boat. I began to persuade myself it was all a delusion, that it was my own foot; I could by no means tell, for certain, where I had walked, and where I had not. If this was only the print of my own foot, I had played the part of those fools who tell ghost stories and frighten themselves more than anybody.

I had not stirred out of my castle for three days and nights, and I had little within doors but some barley-cakes and water. I knew that my goats wanted to be milked; and the poor creatures were in great pain and distress because of it; and, indeed, for some of them it almost dried up their milk.

So I went to my country house to milk my flock. But to see with what fear I went, how often I looked behind me, how I was ready, every now and then, to lay down my basket, and run for my life, it would have made any one think that I had been recently terribly frightened—and so, indeed, I had.

After two or three days, I began to be a little bolder, and to think there was really nothing in it but my own imagination. But I had to go down to the shore again, and see this footprint, and measure it by my own, to be assured it was my own foot. But when I came to the place to compare the print with my own foot, I found my foot not nearly so large. I shook with cold, like one with a fever; and I went home again filled with the belief that some man or men had been on shore there.

Oh, what ridiculous ideas men get when possessed with fear! The first thing I thought of was to throw down my fences, and turn all my tame goats loose so the enemy might not find them; then dig up my two grainfields; then to demolish my bower and tent, that they might not see any sign that I lived there.

Thus fear of danger is ten thousand times more terrifying than danger itself when we can see it; and anxiety is much worse than the evil which we are anxious about. I was like Saul, who complained not only that the Philistines were upon him, but that God had forsaken him. I did not calm myself by crying to God in my distress, and resting upon His providence, as I had done before.

My confusion kept me awake all night, but in the morning I fell asleep exhausted, slept very soundly, and waked much better. And now I reasoned that this island, which was so pleasant, fruitful, and close to the mainland, was not so entirely abandoned as I might imagine, and that there might sometimes come boats from shore. I had lived here fifteen years now, and had not met with the least shadow of any people yet. If at any time they should land here, it was probable they went away again as soon as they possibly could. Therefore, I had nothing to do but to design some safe retreat, in case I should see any savages land.

Now I was sorry that I had dug my cave so large as to make a door out beyond where my wall joined the rock. I decided to make a second wall where I had planted a double row of trees about twelve years before. These trees were so thick that with a few piles driven between them, my new wall would be soon finished.

My outer wall was thickened with pieces of timber, old cables, and everything I could think of to make it strong, having in it seven little holes, about as big as I might put my arm out at, for my seven muskets. I fitted them into frames so I could fire all seven in two minutes' time. I spent many a weary month finishing this wall, and never felt safe till it was done.

When this was done, I planted thousands of young trees outside my wall. Thus in two years' time I had a thick grove; and in five or six years' time I had a wood so thick and strong that it was indeed perfectly impassable. Thus I took all the measures possible for my own preservation.

I had a great concern for my little herd of goats. I could think of only two ways to protect them. One was to dig a cave underground, and to drive them into it every night. The other was to enclose two or three little bits of land, remote from one another where I might keep about half a dozen young goats in each place; so that if any disaster happened to the flock in general, I could replace the flock quickly. And this seemed the best plan.

I finally found a little damp piece of ground, in the middle of the hollow and thick woods where I almost lost myself once trying to come back that way from the eastern part of the island. It was almost an enclosure made by Nature.

18
CANNIBALS

IN LESS THAN A MONTH I had fenced a piece of ground and placed there ten young she-goats and two he-goats. Then I spent more than a month improving the fence.

I did all this on account of the print of a man's foot which I had seen. For two years I had been living uneasily because of that print. And I must admit, with grief, that the terror of falling into the hands of savages had damaged my prayer life. I lived in expectation every night of being murdered and devoured before morning; and I can testify that a mind full of peace, thankfulness, love, and affection is much better for prayer than a mind full of terror. I prayed frantic prayers.

If I had not been cast upon the side of the island where the savages never came, I would have known that when their canoes went a little too far out at sea, they harbored briefly on the west end of the island. Because they were at war, they often had prisoners on board. Being cannibals, they would kill and eat their prisoners before sailing back to the mainland.

One day I wandered farther west than ever before. Looking out to sea from a hill on the southwest point of the island, I thought I saw a boat far away, but I couldn't be sure. I resolved not to go out again without my spyglass in my pocket.

When I came down the hill to the shore, I was horrified. The shore was spread with skulls, hands, feet, and other bones of human bodies. I saw where there had been a fire, and a circle dug in the earth where I suppose the savage wretches had sat down to the inhuman feastings upon the bodies of their fellow-creatures.

I turned away from the horrid spectacle. My stomach grew so sick I almost fainted, but Nature took care of that. Having vomited violently, I was a little relieved, but could not bear to stay there; so I climbed the hill again with all the speed I could, and started to walk home.

On the way, I looked up. With a flood of tears, I gave God thanks that I had not been born among such dreadful creatures as these. I gave thanks, above all, that I had the knowledge of Himself, and the hope of His blessing—a joy that outweighed all the misery I had suffered or could suffer.

I realized that these wretches never came to this island in search of what they could get, evidently not seeking, not wanting, or not expecting, anything here. I had been here now almost eighteen years and never saw the least footsteps of a human creature before; and I might be here eighteen more years entirely concealed from them.

Yet their custom of eating one another made me sad, and I kept close within my own circle for almost two years after this. When I say my own circle, I mean by it my castle, my country home, and my goat paddock in the woods. I went no more to my boat. I was as fearful of seeing the cannibals as of seeing the devil himself.

Eventually I began to live in relaxation as before, only with this difference: I was more cautious, and in order to keep my existence secret, I stopped firing my gun. For two years after this I believe I never fired my gun once, though I never went out without it. I also carried three pistols and had a great broadsword hanging at my side.

I saw more and more how much worse off I could be. How little complaining there would be if people would compare their condition with those that are worse, in order to be thankful, instead of always comparing their condition with those which are better.

Night and day, I could think of nothing but how I might destroy some of these monsters and, if possible, save one of their victims. I thought of digging a hole under the place where they made their fire, and putting in five or six pounds of gunpowder, which, when they kindled their fire, would blow up. But in the first place, I didn't want to waste so much powder upon them, and it might do little more than blow the fire about their ears, and frighten them. Then I thought about ambushing them with gun and sword, and I was so full of this idea that I often dreamed of it.

After making plans for the ambush, I watched for the savages from the top of the hill every morning for two or three months. At last, when I began to weary of this fruitless project, I had cooler and calmer thoughts and began to consider what it was I was doing. What call did I have to be judge and executioner of twenty or thirty naked cannibals? They think it no more a crime to kill a captive taken in war than we do to kill an ox; they think it no more a crime to eat human flesh than we do to eat mutton.

These people were not murderers in the sense that I had condemned them, any more than those Christian soldiers were murderers who frequently destroyed the enemy without mercy even when the enemy was ready to surrender.

I recalled the conduct of the Spaniards in America, where they destroyed millions of native people who had done the Spaniards no harm. Rooting these natives out of the country is spoken of with horror by even the Spaniards themselves at this time, and by all other Christian nations of Europe, as an absolute butchery, unjustifiable either to God or man. For this the very name Spaniard sounds frightful to all people of Christian compassion, as if the kingdom of Spain were made up of a race of men without any tenderness or mercy.

Little by little I began to conclude that while it was not my business to meddle with the savages unless they first attacked me, it was my business, if possible, to prevent an attack. If I were discovered and attacked, then I knew my duty.

I also thought that if only one of them escaped to tell their families what had happened, they might come over again by the thousands to avenge the deaths, and I should have brought upon myself certain destruction.

I felt that if I had committed the thing I planned, it would have been no less a sin than willful murder. I thanked God on my knees that He had saved me from blood-guiltiness. I begged Him to protect me both from falling into the hands of the barbarians and from laying hands on them unless I had a clear call from Heaven to do it in defense of my own life.

19
A SECRET CAVE

FOR ALMOST A YEAR I never went back up the hill to see whether there were any savages in sight, or to know whether any of them had been on shore there. All I did was to move my boat to the east end of the island, where I hid it in a little cove.

I have no doubt that they might have been several times on shore during this period as well as before. Indeed, I considered with horror what my condition would have been if instead of discovering a man's footprint, I had discovered fifteen or twenty savages pursuing me!

This caused me to think more about the dangers we encounter in this life. How wonderfully we are rescued when we know nothing of it. Sometimes, when we might go this way or that way, a secret hint shall direct us this way although we intended to go that way. Sometimes everything tells us to go the other way, yet a strange impression, from we know not where, causes us to go this way; and if we had gone that way as we intended, we should have been ruined and lost. I finally realized this and made it a strict rule to never fail to obey my intuition. 'Tis never too late to be wise.

I no longer wanted to drive a nail, chop a stick of wood, or fire a gun, for fear the noise would be heard. Above all, I was intolerably uneasy about making any fire, lest the smoke, which is visible at a great distance in the daytime, should give me away. But I could not live there without baking my bread, cooking my meat, and firing pots. So I decided to burn some wood near my goat enclosures, as I had seen it done in England, till it became charcoal; and then I carried the coal home, to use for smokeless fire.

I was cutting down some thick branches of trees and brush to make charcoal one day, when I discovered a cave in the earth. I got into the mouth of it with difficulty and found it was large enough for a couple of people to stand upright. But I must confess I made more haste getting out than I did getting in when I saw two broad shining eyes in the darkness, whether devil or man I knew not, reflecting the dim light from the cave's mouth.

After some pause I recovered myself and began to call myself a thousand fools and tell myself he who was afraid to see the devil was not fit to live twenty years on an island all alone. Plucking up my courage, I took up a burning stick, and in I rushed again, with the torch in my hand. I had not gone three steps in when I was almost as much frightened as before; for I heard a very loud sigh, like that of a man in pain, and it was followed by a broken noise, almost like words, and then a deep sigh. It put me into a cold sweat, and if I had had a hat on my head, my hair might have lifted it high. But I told myself that the power and presence of God was everywhere, and was able to protect me, and I stepped forward again. By the light of the torch, holding it up a little over my head, I saw lying on the ground a most monstrous, frightful, old he-goat, just "making his will," as we say, gasping for life and dying of old age.

I stirred him a little to see if I could get him out, and he tried to get up, but was not able to raise himself.

I began to look around and saw that the cave was very small. It might be about twelve feet around, but in no manner of shape, either round or square, no hands having ever been employed in making it but those of Nature. I saw that there was an opening that went in farther, but was so low that it required me to creep upon my hands and knees to go into it. So having no candle, I decided to come again the next day with candles and a tinderbox.

Accordingly, the next day I came provided with six large candles of my own making, for I made very good candles now of goat's tallow. Going into this low place, I was obliged to creep upon all fours, as I have said, almost ten yards; which, by the way, I thought was a venture bold enough, considering that I didn't know how far it might go or what was beyond it. When I had got through the tunnel, I found the roof rose higher up, near twenty feet. But never was such a glorious sight seen in the island, I dare say, as it was, to look round the sides and roof of this cave; the walls reflected a hundred thousand lights to me from my two candles. What it was in the rock, whether diamonds, or other precious stones, or gold, I knew not.

The place was the most delightful cavity or grotto one could find, though perfectly dark. The floor was dry and level and had a sort of small loose gravel upon it. The only difficulty was the small entrance, which suited my purposes perfectly. This is where I would hide most of my weapons and ammunition.

I thought of myself now like one of the ancient giants, which were said to live in caves and holes in the rocks, where none could come at them. I persuaded myself that if five hundred savages were to hunt me, they could never find me here; or, if they did, they would not venture inside to attack me.

The old goat died in the mouth of the cave the day after I found him. As it was easier to dig a great hole there, and throw him in and cover him with earth, than to drag him out, I buried him there, to protect my nose.

I was now in my twenty-third year of residence in this island. I was so used to this manner of living that if I could have been certain that no savages would come to disturb me, I could have been content to have stayed there to the last, till I laid me down and died, like the old goat in the cave. Poll lived with me no less than twenty-six years. How long he might live I know not, though they have a notion in the Brazils that parrots live a hundred years. My dog was a very pleasant and loving companion to me for no less than sixteen years, and then died of old age. As for my cats, when the two old ones I brought with me were gone, I had two or three younger favorites, whose kittens, when they had any, I always drowned. Besides these, I always kept two or three household kids, which I taught to eat out of my hand. And I had two more parrots which talked pretty well and would all call "Robin Crusoe," but none like my first; nor, indeed, did I take the pains with any of them that I had done with him. I had also several tame sea-fowls which I caught upon the shore, and cut their wings. They lived and bred in the grove I had planted before my castle wall, which pleased me. I would have been very well contented with my life, if I had been free from the dread of savages.

Everyone who reads my story would do well to notice how frequently in the course of our lives the evil which we try to avoid—and which, when we are fallen into it, is the most dreadful to us—is the one means by which we can be rescued. This was true of my last years alone on the island.

20
ANOTHER SHIPWRECK

IT WAS NOW THE MONTH of December in my twenty-third year on the island. It was harvest time, and I was working in my fields. Starting out before daylight one morning, I was surprised to see a fire upon the shore about two miles away, on my side of the island.

I rushed back into my castle and pulled up the ladder after me. Then I prepared myself within, loading my muskets and pistols, not forgetting to ask for Divine protection, and earnestly praying to God to deliver me from the savages. I waited about two hours, but began to be mighty impatient for information, for I had no spies to send out.

After musing what I should do, I was not able to bear sitting in ignorance any longer, so I climbed the hill, lay down flat on my belly, and began to look through my spyglass. I presently discovered no less than nine naked savages sitting round a small fire they had made, not for warmth, for they had no need of that in this hot weather, but, I suppose, to cook human flesh they had brought with them—whether alive or dead I do not know.

They had two canoes with them, which they had hauled up on the shore; and as it was then ebb tide, they seemed to be waiting for flood tide so they could go away again. As I expected, so it proved; for as soon as the tide shifted, I saw them all embark and paddle away. For over an hour before they left, they were dancing, stark naked.

As soon as they were gone, I armed myself and hurried to the hill where I had first discovered them. It took me two hours to get there, and I saw that there had been three canoes full there. Now they were all at sea heading back to the mainland.

Going down to the shore, I could see the marks of horror they had left behind: the blood, the bones, and parts of human bodies, devoured by those wretches as if at a party. I was so filled with indignation at the sight that I planned to kill the next savage I saw.

It was more than fifteen months before any of them came on shore there again; in the rainy seasons, they don't venture far. Yet all this while I lived in fear. The expectation of evil is more bitter than the suffering, especially if there is no relief from it.

During all this time I was in a mood for murder, and took up most of my hours, which should have been better used, in planning how to attack them, especially if they should be divided again into two parties. I didn't consider that if I killed one party, suppose ten or a dozen, I was still the next day, or week, or month, to kill another, and so on indefinitely, till I should be at length no less a murderer than they were, and perhaps much more so.

I wore out a year and three months before I saw any more of the savages. In the month of May, as near as I could calculate, in my twenty-fourth   year on the island, I had a very strange encounter with them, which I will tell later.

During this fifteen or sixteen month interval I slept poorly, dreamed frightful dreams, and often awoke with a start during the night. It was in the middle of May, on the sixteenth day, I think, as well as my poor wooden calendar would reckon, that there came a very great storm of wind all day, with a great deal of lightning and thunder, and followed by a stormy night. As I was reading in the Bible, I was surprised by the noise of a gun that sounded as if it were fired at sea.

I jumped up in the greatest haste imaginable, and got to the top of the hill in time to see the flash of a fired gun, which I heard in about half a minute. By the sound, I knew that it was from that part of the sea where I had been driven east along the current in my boat.

I immediately figured that this must be some ship in distress, and that they had fired these guns as signals for help. Although I could not help them, perhaps they might help me; so I brought together all the dry wood I could get quickly, and set it on fire upon the hill. The wood was dry and blazed freely although the wind blew very hard, so that I was certain, if there was any such thing as a ship, they must see it. No doubt they did, for as soon as my fire blazed up I heard another gun, and after that several others. I tended my fire till day broke, then I saw something at a great distance in the sea, whether a sail or a hull I could not distinguish in the sea haze.

It did not move all day, so I concluded it was a ship at an anchor. I eagerly took my gun in my hand and ran toward the south side of the island, to the rocks where I had formerly been carried away by the current. Getting up there, I could plainly see, to my great sorrow, the wreck of a ship, destroyed in the night upon those concealed rocks which I found when I was out in my boat. Those very rocks, which had created a kind of eddy, had rescued me from the most dangerous situation of my whole life.

Thus, what is one man's safety is another man's destruction. It seems these men, whoever they were, had been driven upon the rocks in the night. After that, several things could have happened to them. Perhaps they saw my fire and perished while trying to get to shore in a small boat. Perhaps their small boat was already washed overboard. Perhaps another ship saved them and carried them away. Perhaps the current swept them out to sea in their small boat, and they would slowly starve to death and eat one another.

There was nothing I could do but pity the poor men. This had the good effect of giving me more and more cause to give thanks to God, who had so happily and comfortably provided for me in my desolate condition. I learned again that there is rarely any condition of life so low, or any misery so great, but we may see something or other to be thankful for, and may see others in worse circumstances than our own.

I cannot explain what a strange longing I felt in my soul now, breaking out sometimes like this: "If only there had been one soul saved out of this ship, to have escaped to me, so I might but have had one companion, one fellow-creature, to talk with!" In all my years alone, I never felt so strong a desire for the company of fellow-creatures.

21
WONDERFUL DREAM

"IF ONLY ONE MAN HAD SURVIVED!" I believe I repeated the words a thousand times. I spoke the words with my hands clenched, my fingers pressed into my palms, and my teeth in my head clenched together.

But it was not to be. Either their fate or mine, or both, forbid it. I never knew whether any were saved out of that ship or not; but I had the grief, a few days after the wreck, to see the corpse of a drowned boy come on shore at the end of the island near the shipwreck. He had nothing in his pocket but two gold coins and a tobacco-pipe. The last was to me ten times more valuable than the first.

It was calm now, and I had a great mind to venture out in my boat to' this wreck, not doubting but I might find something on board that would be useful to me. Better yet, there might be some living creature on board whose life I might save, and might, by saving that life, comfort my own. This thought clung to my heart night and day. The impression was so strong upon my mind that I felt I would be wrong if I did not go.

I hastened back to my castle, prepared everything for my voyage, took a quantity of bread, a great pot for fresh water, a compass to steer by, a bottle of rum (for I had still a great deal of that left), and a basket full of raisins. And thus, loading myself with everything necessary,

I went down to my boat, got the water out of her, got her afloat, loaded all my cargo in her, and then went home again for more. My second cargo was a great bag full of rice, the umbrella to set up over my head for shade, another large pot full of fresh water, and about two dozen of my small loaves, or barley-cakes, more than before, with a bottle of goat's milk and a cheese. All of this, with great labor and sweat, I brought to my boat. Praying to God to direct my voyage, I put out, paddling the canoe along the shore.

I came at last to the northeast point of the island, and now I was to launch out into the ocean. I looked at the distant currents, and my heart began to fail me; for I foresaw that if I was driven into either of those currents, I should be carried a vast way out to sea.

Having hauled my boat into a little creek on the shore, I stepped out, and sat down nearby, torn between fear and desire. As I was musing, I could see that the tide was turned, and it occurred to me that should I go up to the highest piece of ground, I could find and observe the currents. I did so, and discovered that if I kept to the north of the island on my return, I should be safe enough.

Encouraged with this observation, I decided to set out the next morning with the first of the tide. The eastward current carried me at a great rate, and in less than two hours I came up to the wreck.

It was a dismal sight to look at. The ship, which looked Spanish, was jammed in between two rocks. All the stern and quarter of her was beaten to pieces by the sea. Her forecastle, which stuck in the rocks, had met with violence great enough to break off her mainmast and foremast. But her bowsprit was sound, and the head and bow appeared firm. When I came close to her a dog appeared, who yelped and cried. As soon as I called him, he jumped into the sea to come to me. I took him into the boat and found him almost dead from hunger and thirst. I gave him bread, and he ate it like a ravenous wolf that had been starving two weeks in the snow. I then gave the poor creature some fresh water, with which, if I had let him, he would have burst himself.

After this I went on board, and my first sight was of two men drowned in the cook-room. I concluded that during the storm, the waves broke so high, and so continually, that the men were strangled with the constant rushing in of the water, as if they had been entirely under water. Besides the dog, there was nothing left in the ship that had life, nor any cargo that wasn't spoiled by water. There were some casks of liquor, whether wine or brandy I knew not, which I could see, but they were too big to meddle with. I saw several chests which I believed belonged to some of the seamen. I got two of them into the boat, without examining what was in them.

From what I found in these two chests, I suppose the ship had a great deal of wealth on board. And if I may guess by the course she steered, she must have been bound from Buenos Aires in the south part of America, beyond the Brazils, to Havana, in the Gulf of Mexico, and so perhaps to Spain. She had, no doubt, a great treasure in her.

I found, besides these chests, several muskets in a cabin, and a great powder-horn, with about four pounds of powder in it. As for the muskets, I had no occasion for them, so I left them, but took the powder-horn. I also took a fire-shovel and tongs, which I wanted badly, as well as two little brass kettles, a copper pot to make chocolate, and a gridiron. With this cargo, and the dog, I came away, the tide beginning to change again. The same evening I reached the island, weary and fatigued to the last degree.

I slept that night in my boat. In the morning I decided to stash in my cave what I had gotten, rather than carrying it home to my castle. After refreshing myself, I got all my cargo on shore, and began to examine it. When I came to open the chests, I found several things of great use to me. For example, I found in one a fine case of bottles, of an extraordinary kind, and filled with fine cordial waters; the bottles held about three pints each, and were tipped with silver. I found two pots of very good sweetmeats, and two more of the same which the water had spoiled. I found some very good shirts, which were much

131

welcome, and about a dozen and half of white linen handkerchiefs and colored neck-cloths. The former were also very welcome, being exceeding refreshing to wipe my face on a hot day. Besides this, I found three great bags of pieces of eight, about eleven hundred pieces in all. In one of them, wrapped up in a paper, I found six doubloons of gold, and some small bars or wedges of gold. I suppose they might all weigh nearly a pound.

The other chest contained some poor clothes and a little gunpowder. Upon the whole, I got little from this voyage that was of any use to me. As to the money, I had no use for it; it was like the dirt under my feet, and I would have given it all for three or four pair of English shoes and stockings, which were things I greatly wanted, but had not had on my feet now for many years. I had indeed gotten two pair of shoes which I took off of the feet of the two drowned men whom I saw in the wreck, and I found two pair more in one of the chests; but they were not like our English shoes, either for comfort or service. I found in this chest about fifty pieces of eight in royals, but no gold. I suppose this belonged to a poorer man than the other, which seemed to belong to some officer.

I lugged this money home to my cave, as I had done earlier with the money which I brought from our own ship. It was great pity that the other part of this ship had not come to my shore, for I am sure I might have loaded my canoe several times over with money, which, if I had ever escaped to England, would have been safe here till I could come again and fetch it.

For a while, I lived easy enough, although I was more vigilant than I used to be, looked out more often, and did not travel much. If at any time I enjoyed an outing, it was always to the east part of the island, where I was pretty well satisfied the savages never came and where I could go without so many precautions, and such a load of arms and ammunition as I always carried with me if I went to the west.

I lived in this condition nearly two years more; but my unlucky head, that was born to make my body miserable, was always filled with projects and designs for getting away from this island.

I have always been a monument for those who are touched with the general plague of mankind, from which, I suspect, one-half of their miseries flow: I mean not being satisfied with the situation where God and Nature had placed them. Looking back at my beginning and the excellent advice of my father, my discontent there was, as I may call it, my original sin. If Providence, which placed me in the Brazils as a planter, had blessed me with contentment, I might by now have become one of the most successful planters in the Brazils. I am persuaded that if I had stayed, I might have become a millionaire. What business had I to leave a fine plantation to sail to Guinea to fetch Negro slaves, when we could have bought them at our own door from those whose business it was to fetch them?

But as foolishness is typical of young heads, so reflection about folly is typical of age or of costly experience. So it was with me. And yet, so deep was discontent rooted in me, that I was continually considering the possibility of escape from this place. So that the reader may have greater pleasure in the remaining part of my story, here is an account of my foolish scheme for my escape, and how, and upon what foundation, I acted.

I had retired into my castle, after my recent voyage to the wreck. I had more wealth, indeed, than I had before, but was not at all the richer, for I had no more use for gold than the Indians of Peru had before the Spaniards came there.

It was one of the nights in the rainy season in March, the twenty-fourth year of my first setting foot in this island. I was lying in my hammock, awake, very well in health, had no pain, no discomfort, no, nor any uneasiness of mind, or any more than ordinary, but could by no means close my eyes to sleep. No, not a wink all night long, otherwise than as follows.

It is impossible to set down the crowd of thoughts that whirled through that great thoroughfare of the brain, my memory, in this one night. I ran over the whole condensed history of my life to my coming to this island, and also of the part of my life since I came to this island. I compared my happy years here to the life of anxiety and fear which I had lived ever since I had seen the print of a foot in the sand. I had been as happy in not knowing my danger, as if I had never had any danger. How infinitely good it is that Providence has limited mankind's sight and knowledge of things. Although we walk in the midst of so many thousand dangers, we are kept serene and calm by having things hid from our eyes, and knowing nothing of the dangers which surround us.

I had walked about in the greatest security, and with all possible tranquility, when perhaps nothing but a brow of a hill, a great tree, or the approach of night had been between me and the cannibals who would have seized me the same as I seized a goat or a turtle, and would have thought it no more a crime to kill me, than I did to kill a pigeon. I would slander myself if I should say I was not sincerely thankful to my great Preserver.

My head was for some time taken up in considering these wretched savages, and how the Creator could give up any of His creatures to behavior worse than brutality. But after this speculation, I began to wonder where they came from, why they came, and what kind of boats they had. Why couldn't I go to the mainland?

I didn't consider what I should do with myself when I got there, because I was so excited by the notion of going to the mainland. I felt that only death could be worse than my present condition. I might come to some inhabited country, or some Christian ship that might take me in; and if worse came to worst, I could die and put an end to all my miseries at once. Please understand that all this was the fruit of a disturbed mind made desperate by the disappointments of the wreck. I had been so near to obtaining somebody to speak to, and to learning where I was and how I might get away. All my calm trust in

Providence seemed to have disappeared.

I was so agitated for about two hours that my pulse beat as fast as if I had a fever. Then, exhausted from thinking, Nature threw me into a sound sleep. One would have thought I should have dreamed of sailing to the mainland, but I did not. I dreamed that as I was going out in the morning, as usual, from my castle, I saw upon the shore two canoes and eleven savages coming to land, and that they brought with them another savage, whom they were going to kill and eat. All of a sudden, the victim jumped away and ran for his life. And I thought, in my sleep, that he came running into my thick grove to hide; and I, seeing him alone, showed myself to him, and smiled upon him. He kneeled down to me, seeming to beg for help, whereupon I showed him my ladder, made him go up, and carried him into my cave, and he became my servant. I said to myself, "Now I may certainly venture to the mainland, for this fellow will serve me as a pilot and a guide." I waked with this thought, and had such inexpressible joy at the prospect of my escape that when I found it was no more than a dream I was thrown into a great depression.

From this, however, I decided that my only way to attempt an escape was, if possible, to get a savage into my possession. Also if possible, it should be one of their prisoners whom they had condemned to be eaten. But it was impossible to accomplish this without attacking a whole caravan of them, and killing them all. Not only was this a very desperate attempt, and might fail, but also my heart trembled at the thought of shedding so much blood, though it was for my deliverance. I could justify it with arguments, but I could not reconcile myself to it.

At last, after many secret disputes with myself, and after great perplexities about it, I resolved, if possible, to get one of those savages into my hands, cost what it would. I resolved to put myself upon the watch, to see them when they came on shore, and leave the rest to the event, let be what would be.

For more than a year and half I waited, and for a great part of that time I went out to the west end of the island almost every day, looking for canoes, but none appeared. The longer the arrival seemed to be delayed, the more eager I was for it. I had never been so careful to avoid these savages as I was now eager to encounter them.

Besides, I imagined myself able to enslave two or three savages, if I had them, to do whatever I wanted, and to prevent their being able to do me any harm. All my fancies and schemes came to nothing, however, for no savages came near me for a great while.

22
FINDING FRIDAY

ABOUT A YEAR AND A HALF after I had formed my desperate plan, I was surprised, one morning early, to see no less than five canoes all on shore together on my side of the island, and the people in them already landed and out of my sight. Knowing that they always came four, or six, or sometimes more, in a boat, I could not tell what to think of it, or how to attack twenty or thirty men single-handed, so I armed myself and waited quietly for a long time. At length, being very impatient, I set my guns at the foot of my ladder and clambered up to the top of the hill. There I observed, by the help of my spyglass, that they were no less than thirty in number, that they had a fire kindled, that they had food prepared. How they had cooked it, that I knew not, or what it was. But they were all dancing in their own wild way round the fire.

While I was thus looking, I saw two miserable wretches dragged from the boats for slaughter. One of them immediately fell, being knocked down, I suppose, with a club or wooden sword, and two or three others were at work immediately, cutting him open for their cookery. The other victim was left standing by himself till they should be ready for him. In that very moment this poor wretch darted away from them, and ran with incredible swiftness along the sands directly toward my home.

I was dreadfully frightened (that I must acknowledge) when I saw him run my way, and especially when, as I thought, I saw him pursued by all the rest; and now I expected that part of my dream was coming to pass, and that he would certainly take shelter in my grove. But I could not depend, by any means, upon my dream that the other savages would not pursue him there and find him. However, my spirits began to recover when I found that only three men followed him. I was encouraged further when I found that he outran them.

When the savage came to the creek, he made nothing of it, but plunged in, swam across, and ran on with great strength and swiftness. When the three others came to the creek, the third could not swim and came no farther.

I saw that the two who swam took twice as long swimming over the creek as the fellow who was fleeing. Now was my time to get a servant, and perhaps a companion or assistant, and I was called plainly by Providence to save this poor creature's life. I immediately fetched my two guns and ran back to the top of the hill, then ran down hill and came out between the pursuers and the pursued. I yelled to the victim, and at first he was perhaps as much frightened of me as of them. I beckoned with my hand for him to come back, and in the meantime, I started toward his pursuers. I knocked the first one down with the butt of my gun, being unwilling to fire. The second one stopped, and as I approached him I saw he was preparing to shoot me with his bow and arrow. So I shot him dead.

The poor savage I was saving stood stock-still, and neither came forward nor went backward, although he looked inclined to run.

I called and signaled for him to come, which he easily understood. He came a little way, then stopped, then a little farther, and stopped again. He stood trembling, as if he had been taken prisoner and was going to be killed. I beckoned, and he came nearer and nearer, kneeling down every ten or twelve steps, in acknowledgement for my saving his life. I smiled and beckoned to him to come still nearer. At length he came close to me, and then he kneeled down, laid his head upon the ground, and taking me by the foot, set my foot upon his head. He seemed to be swearing to be my slave forever. I got him up and encouraged him, but then I saw the one whom I knocked down beginning to come to himself. So I pointed to him, and the savage spoke some words to me. Though I could not understand them, they were the first sound of a human voice that I had heard, except for my own, for over twenty-five years.

But this was no time for reflection. The savage on the ground sat up and I aimed my other gun at him. At this, my savage, for so I call him now, motioned for my sword, which hung naked by my side. He no sooner had it but he ran to his enemy and cut off his head at one blow. No executioner in Germany could have done it faster or better. I learned afterwards that they make their wooden swords so sharp and so heavy that they will cut off heads and arms at one blow. When he had done this, he came to me in triumph, and laid down the sword and the head of the savage before me.

He pointed to the savage I had shot and made signs to me to let him go to look. He was amazed, turned the body first on one side, then the other, and looked at the bullet hole. It had pierced his breast and he had bled inwardly, for he was quite dead. I beckoned to my savage to follow me because more might come after us.

He signaled that he should bury them with sand that they might not be found, and so I agreed. In an instant he had scraped a hole in the sand with his hands big enough to bury the first, and then dragged him into it, and covered him. So he did with the other. I believe he buried them both in a quarter of an hour. Then I led him away to my secret cave on the far part of the island. Thus I did not let my dream come true that he came into my grove for shelter.

I gave him bread and a bunch of raisins and a drink of water, and made signs for him to lie down on a mat of rice-straw with a blanket upon it, where I used to sleep sometimes. So the poor creature lay down and went to sleep.

He was a handsome fellow with straight, strong limbs, tall and well-shaped, and about twenty-six years of age. He had a very manly face, and yet he had all the sweetness and softness of a European in his face too, especially when he smiled. His hair was long and black, his forehead very large, and a sparkling sharpness in his eyes. The color of his skin was tawny and very agreeable, though not very easy to describe. His face was round and plump, his nose small, but not flat, a very good mouth with thin lips, and fine teeth, white as ivory.

After about half an hour, he waked again, and came out of the cave to me, for I had been milking my goats. He came running to me, laying himself down again upon the ground, with all the possible signs of a humble, thankful disposition. I understood him and let him know I was very well pleased with him. I began to teach him to speak to me and let him know his name should be Friday, which was the day I saved his life. I taught him to say master, and then let him know that was to be my name. I also taught him to say yes and no, and what they meant. I gave him some milk in an earthen pot, and let him see me drink some and sop my bread in it, and he quickly copied me and made signs that he liked it.

I kept him there all night, then I beckoned for him to come with me to get some clothes, which made him glad, for he was stark naked. As we went by the place where he had buried the two men, he made signs to me that we should dig them up again and eat them. At this I expressed great anger and showed that I might vomit at the thought of it, and led him away.

The savages and their canoes were gone. Friday carried my sword and one of my guns for me, with the bow and arrows on his back, and away we marched to the place where the savages had been feasting. When we got there, my blood ran chill in my veins, and my heart sank within me at the horror of the spectacle, although Friday made nothing of it. The place was covered with human bones, the ground dyed with blood, great pieces of flesh left here and there, half-eaten, mangled,

I began to teach him to speak to me and let him know
his name should be Friday, which was the day I saved his life.

and scorched. I saw three skulls, five hands, the bones of three or four legs and feet, and abundance of other parts of the bodies. Friday made me understand that they brought over four prisoners to feast upon. Three of them were eaten up, and he was the fourth. There had been a great battle between two neighboring kingdoms, and the winners had captured a great number of prisoners to feast upon.

I caused Friday to gather all the remains into a heap and burn them all to ashes. I could tell he had a hankering for some of the meat and was still a cannibal; but he realized I would not tolerate it.

When we came back to our castle, I gave him a pair of linen trousers from the poor gunner's chest in the wreck. Then I made him a vest of goat's skin, for I was now a tolerably good tailor. And I gave him a cap, which I had made of a hare-skin, very convenient and fashionable. He was mighty well pleased to see himself almost as well clothed as his master. It is true he was uncomfortable at first, but with a little stretching where they were tight, and getting used to them, he came to like his clothes very well.

I made a little tent for Friday in the space between my two walls. I made sure that he could in no way approach me in the inside of my innermost wall without making so much noise in getting over that I would awaken. As to weapons, I took them all in with me every night.

But I needed none of this precaution. Never man had a more faithful, loving, sincere servant than Friday was to me. His very affections were set on me like those of a child to a father. I dare say he would have sacrificed his life to save mine, upon any occasion whatsoever.

Although it has pleased God, in His providence, to deprive so many of His creatures of the opportunity to use their higher gifts, yet He has bestowed upon them the same talents, the same reason, the same affections, the same sense of kindness and obligation, the same resentment of wrong, the same sense of gratitude, sincerity, faithfulness, and all the capacities of doing good and receiving good that He has given to us. And when they get the chance, they are more ready to use these gifts well than we are. It made me sad sometimes to think of what poor use we make of our gifts, even though we have the Spirit of God and knowledge of His Word. I don't know why it has pleased God to hide saving knowledge from so many millions of souls who, if I might judge by this poor savage, would make much better use of it than we do.

I decided that as God is by nature infinitely holy and just, so it must be that if these creatures were all sentenced to separation from God, it was on account of sinning against that light which they had, and by breaking such rules as their consciences would acknowledge to be just.

Also, that if we are all clay in the hands of the potter, we should not say to Him, "Why hast Thou formed me thus?"

But to return to my new companion. I was delighted with him and taught him to be useful, handy, and helpful, but especially to make him speak and understand me. He was the best student there ever was, and was so merry, so constantly diligent, and so pleased when he could understand me, or make me understand him, that it was a pleasure to talk to him. And now my life was so happy that if I could have been safe from more savages, I wouldn't care if I never left the island alive.

23

FRIENDSHIP

AFTER TWO OR THREE DAYS back at my castle, I thought that in order to change Friday's cannibal stomach, I ought to let him taste other meat. Therefore I took him out with me one morning to the woods intending to kill a kid out of my own flock, but on the way, I saw a she-goat lying down in the shade with two young kids sitting by her. I caught hold of Friday. "Hold," says I, "stand still," and made signs to him not to stir. Immediately I took aim and shot one of the kids. The poor man, who had at a distance seen me kill his enemy, but did not know how it was done, trembled and shook, and looked so shocked, that I thought he would collapse. He did not see the kid I had killed, but yanked up his vest to feel if he was wounded; and then he kneeled down to me, embracing my knees, and I could easily see that he was begging me not to kill him.

Taking him up by the hand, I laughed at him, and pointing to the kid which I had killed, beckoned to him to run and fetch it, which he did. I loaded my gun again, and by and by I saw a great parrot in a tree. So, to let Friday understand a little what I would do, I called him to me again, pointing to the parrot and to my gun, and to the ground under the parrot, to let him see I would make it fall. Accordingly I fired, and he saw the parrot fall. The astonishment this created in him would not wear off for a long time. I believe, if I had let him, he would have worshiped me and my gun. As for the gun itself, he would not so much as touch it for several days after, but would talk to it and ask it not to kill him.

That day I boiled some of the meat from the kid, and made some very good broth. After I had begun to eat some, I gave some to my man, who liked it very well. But while I ate salt with it, he liked it without salt.

I decided to give him a feast the next day by roasting a piece of the kid on a turning spit over the fire. Friday admired this, and when he tasted the meat, he told me in sign language that he would never eat human flesh again, which I was very glad to hear.

The next day I set him to work preparing flour, and in a little time Friday was able to do all the work for making bread as well as I could do it myself. Having two mouths to feed instead of one, I needed to plant more grain than before, so I began to fence in more field. Friday let me know that he thought I had much more labor on his account than I had by myself, and that he would work all the harder for me if I would tell him what to do.

This was my most pleasant year on the island. Friday began to talk pretty well, and understand the names of almost everything I had occasion to call for and of every place I had to send him, and to talk a great deal to me. Besides the pleasure of talking to him, I had a great pleasure in the fellow himself. His simple honesty appeared to me more and more every day, and we really loved each other.

Having taught him English so well that he could answer almost any question, I asked him whether the nation he belonged to never conquered in battle. He smiled, and said, "Yes, yes, we always fight the better!" So we began the following conversation: "If you always fight the better," said I, "how were you taken prisoner then, Friday?"

Friday: "They more many than my nation in the place where me was; they take one, two, three, and me. My nation overbeat them in the yonder place, where me no was. There my nation take one, two, great thousand."

Master: "But why didn't your side rescue you from the hands of your enemies?"

Friday: "They run one, two, three and me, and make go in the canoe; my nation have no canoe that time."

Master: "Well, Friday, what does your nation do with people they capture? Do they carry them away and eat them also?"

Friday: "Yes, my nation eat mans too; eat all up."

Master: "Do they come to this island?"

Friday: "Yes, yes, they come here; come other else place."

Master. "Have you been here with them?"

Friday: "Yes, I been here." (He points to the northwest.)

Some time later, when I had the courage to carry him to that side of the island, he knew the place, and told me he was there once when they ate up twenty men, two women, and one child. He could not say twenty in English, but he lay that many stones in a row.

I asked him how far it was from our island to the mainland, and whether the canoes were not often lost. He told me there was no danger, no canoes were ever lost because there was a current and a wind, always one way in the morning, the other in the afternoon.

I later learned that our island lay in the gulf of the mighty river Orinoco, and the mainland I saw in the northwest was the great island of Trinidad, on the north point of the mouth of the river. I asked Friday a thousand questions about the country, the inhabitants, the sea, the coast, and what nations were near. He told me all he knew, with the greatest openness imaginable. I understood that these were the Caribbees, which our maps place on the part of America which reaches from the mouth of the river Orinoco to Guiana, and onward to St. Martha. He told me that up a great way beyond the moon (beyond the setting of the moon, which means west) there dwelt white-bearded men, like me, and that they had killed much mans. I understood he meant the Spaniards, whose cruelties were remembered by all the tribes from father to son.

I inquired if he could tell me how I might get to those white men. He told me, "Yes, yes, I might go in two canoe." At last, with great difficulty, I found he meant it must be in a large boat, as big as two canoes. From this time on I had hopes that sooner or later I might find an opportunity to make my escape from this place, and this poor savage might help me to do it.

Ever since Friday began to understand me, I was laying a foundation of religious knowledge in his mind. I asked him one time who made him. The poor creature thought I had asked who was his father. But I took it by another handle, and asked him who made the sea, the ground we walked on, and the hills and woods. He told me it was one old Benamuckee, that lived beyond all. He could describe nothing of this great person, but that he was very old, much older than the sea or the land, than the moon or the stars. I asked him if this old person had made all things, why did not all things worship him? With a perfect look of innocence, he said, "All things do say O to him." I asked him if the people who die in his country went away anywhere. He said, "Yes, they all go to Benamuckee." Then I asked him whether people they ate up went there too? He said, "Yes."

From these things I began to instruct him about the true God. He listened with great attention, and received with pleasure the notion of Jesus Christ being sent to redeem us, and how to make our prayers to God, and His being able to hear us in heaven. He told me one day that our God must be greater than their Benamuckee, who could not hear till they went up to the great mountains where he dwelt. I asked him if he ever went there to speak to him. He said no, none went there but the old men called Oowokakee, who went to say O (so he called saying prayers) and then came back and told people what Benamuckee said. I realized then that false priests are common even among the most brutish savages.

I tried to clear up this fraud to my man Friday, and told him that their old men going up to the mountains to say O to Benamuckee was a cheat, and their bringing back what he said was much more so; that if the priests met with any answer, or spoke with any one there, it must be with an evil spirit. Then I started telling him about the devil, his rebellion against God, his enmity to man, the reason for it, his setting himself up in the dark parts of the world to be worshiped instead of God, and his many ways to delude mankind into ruin.

I had been telling him how the devil was God's enemy in the hearts of men and used all his skill to ruin the kingdom of Christ in the world. "Well," says Friday, "but you say God is so strong, so great; is He no much strong, much might as the devil?" "Yes, yes," says I. "Friday, God is stronger than the devil; God is above the devil, and therefore we pray to God to tread him down under our feet, and enable us to resist his temptation, and quench his fiery darts." "But," says he again, "if God much strong, much might as the devil, why God no kill the devil, so make him no more do wicked?"

At first I didn't know what to say, so I pretended not to hear him, and asked him what he said. But he repeated his question in the very same broken words. By this time I had recovered a little, and I said, "God will punish him severely; he is to be cast into the bottomless pit, to dwell with everlasting fire." This did not satisfy Friday. "Me no understand. Why not kill the devil now? Not kill great ago?" "You may as well ask me," said I, "why God does not kill you and me, when we do wicked things. We are given time to repent and be pardoned." "Well," he said joyfully, "that well; so you, I, devil, all wicked, all repent, God pardon all."

I rose up suddenly, and sent him on a long errand. Then I seriously prayed to God that He would help me to teach this poor savage and would guide me to speak to him from the Word of God such as his conscience might be touched, his eyes opened, and his soul saved. When he came back, I talked with him about repentance toward God, and faith in our blessed Lord Jesus. I had, God knows, more sincerity than knowledge in laying things open to him. I taught myself many things that either I did not know or had not fully considered. And I was more motivated than ever before.

So whether this poor, wild wretch was helped by me or not, I had great reason to be thankful to him. My grief set lighter upon me. In this isolated life, I had not only been moved to look up to heaven to seek the hand that had brought me there, but I was now an instrument to save the life, and, for all I know, the soul of a poor savage, and bring him to the true knowledge of Christianity, that he might know Christ Jesus, whom to know is life eternal. When I reflected upon all these things, a secret joy ran through every part of my soul, and I often rejoiced that I was brought to this place, which I had so often thought the worst thing that could have befallen me.

The conversations between Friday and me made the three years which we lived there together perfectly and completely happy, if complete happiness can exist on this earth. He was now a good Christian, much better than I. We had the Word of God to read and were no farther off from His Spirit than if we had been in England.

I read the Bible and let him know, as well as I could, the meaning of what I read; and he, by his serious questions, made me a much better Bible student than I should ever have been on my own. Reading the Bible had caused me to repent for my sins, trust my Savior, reform my character, and obey God's commands, all without any human teacher. So the same plain Bible teaching turned this savage into such a Christian that I have known few equal to him in my life.

As to all the worlds' wranglings, battles, and confusion about religion, whether details of belief or church business, they were all perfectly useless to us—as, for all I can see, they have been useless to everyone. We had the Word of God, and we had the Spirit of God teaching and instructing us by His Word. But I must go on with what happened, in the order in which it happened.

150

24
ARRIVAL OF SAVAGES

AFTER FRIDAY COULD SPEAK FLUENTLY to me in broken English, I told him my story: about my coming there, how I had survived, and for how long. I let him into the mystery of gunpowder and bullet, and taught him how to shoot. I gave him a knife, which he was wonderfully delighted with, and I made him a belt, with a loop for hanging a hatchet.

I described Europe, and particularly England, which I came from; how we lived, how we worshiped God, how we behaved to one another, and how we traded in ships around the world. I described my shipwreck and showed him the place, but she was long beaten to pieces and gone.

I showed him the ruins of the small lifeboat, now fallen almost all to pieces. When he saw it, Friday stood musing and said nothing. At last he said, "Me see such boat like come to place at my nation. We save the white mans from drown." I asked him if there were any white mans, as he called them, in the boat. "Yes," he said, "the boat full of white mans." I asked him how many. He showed on his fingers: seventeen. I asked him then what became of them. He told me, "They live at my nation."

This made me wonder if these might be the men wrecked near my island. I asked more, and he said they had been there about four

151

years and that his people let them alone and gave them food. I asked why they didn't kill them and eat them. He said, "No, they make brother with them." Then he added, "They no eat mans but when make the war fight."

One clear day on the top of the hill on the east side of the island, Friday looked toward the mainland and began jumping and dancing. "O joy! O glad! There see my country, there my nation!" His eyes sparkled.

It suddenly occurred to me that if Friday could get back to his own nation again, he would forget all his religion and all his obligation to me. He would tell his countrymen about me, and come back perhaps with a hundred or two of them, and feast upon me.

I wronged the poor honest creature very much, for which I was very sorry afterwards. But my jealousy increased, and I was less friendly and kind to him. This was wrong, because the honest, grateful creature was both a Christian and my friend. You may be sure I was every day checking him, but everything he said was so honest and so innocent that I could find nothing to feed my suspicion.

One hazy day I said, "Friday, do you wish yourself in your own country, your own nation?" "Yes," he said, "I be much O glad to be at my own nation." "Would you turn wild again, eat men's flesh again, and be a savage as you were before?" He shook his head and said, "No, no; Friday tell them to live good; tell them to pray God; tell them to eat bread, cattle-meat, milk, no eat man again." I said, "Then they will kill you." He looked grave at that, and then said, "No, they no kill me, they willing love learn." He meant they were willing to learn, and added that they learned much from the bearded mans that come in the boat. I asked him if he would go back to them, and told me with a chuckle he could not swim so far. I offered to make a canoe, and he told me he would go if I would go with him. "I go?" says I; "why, they will eat me if I come there." "No, no," says he, "me make they no eat you; me make they much love you."

152

From this time on I had a mind to venture over and see if I could possibly join with the bearded men, who were probably Spaniards or Portuguese. So I told Friday I would give him a boat to go back to his own nation, and I took him to my canoe which lay on the other side of the island. I always kept it sunk in the water, so I brought it out and we tried it. He could make it go almost as swift and fast as I could. I said to him, "Well now, Friday, shall we go to your nation?" He looked glum because he thought the boat too small to go so far.

I told him then I had a bigger one. The next day I went to the place where the first boat lay which I had made, which I could not get into the water. He said it was big enough, but it had lain over twenty-two years there, and the wood was rotten. Friday told me that size would do very well, and would carry "much enough" food and drink.

I told him we would make one as big as that, and he should go home in it. He answered, "Why you angry mad with Friday? What me done?" I told him I was not angry with him at all. "Why send Friday home away to my nation?" Says I, "Friday, did you not say you wished you were there?" "Yes, yes," says he, "wish be both there." In a word, he would not think of going there without me. I tested him, "No, no, Friday, you shall go without me. Leave me here to live by myself, as I did before." He looked confused, ran for a hatchet, and gave it me. "What must I do with this?" I asked. "You take kill Friday, no send Friday away." I saw tears in his eyes. So I told him then, and often after, that I would never send him away.

His desire to go to his own country lay in his affection for the people and his hopes of my doing them good, a thing which didn't interest me. But I wanted to go there to meet the seventeen bearded men. Therefore without any more delay I went to work with Friday to find a great tree to make into a canoe for the voyage. The main thing I wanted was one so near the water that we might launch it when it was made, to avoid the mistake I committed at first.

In about a month's hard labor we finished the canoe, and made it very handsome. After this, it took us nearly two weeks to get her, inch by inch, upon great rollers, into the water. When she was in, she would have carried twenty men with great ease.

Next I wanted a mast and sail, an anchor and cable, which took nearly two months. After all this was done, I taught Friday navigation, for though he well knew how to paddle a canoe, he knew nothing about a sail and a rudder. He became an expert sailor, except that I couldn't make him understand the compass. In those parts there was little use for a compass, because there was very little cloudy weather. The stars were always to be seen by night, and the shore by day, except in the rainy seasons, and then nobody cared to go out, either by land or sea.

I was entering the twenty-seventh year of my captivity in this place, though the three years I had this creature with me should not be counted, being different from the rest of the time. I observed again the anniversary of my landing here with the same thankfulness to God for His mercies as at first. Now I felt strongly that my deliverance was at hand, and that I should not be another year in this place. However, I went on digging, planting, fencing, as usual. I gathered and dried my grapes and did everything as before.

The rainy season was upon us, so we stowed and docked our new vessel up the creek, and covered her thickly with tree boughs. Thus we waited for November and December for our adventure.

I was busy one morning preparing for the trip, when I called to Friday and sent him to find a turtle, something we generally got once a week for the eggs as well as the meat. Friday had not been long gone when he came running back and flew over my outer wall like one whose feet didn't touch the ground. Before I had time to speak to him, he cried out to me, "O master! O master! O sorrow! O bad! O yonder, there, one, two, three canoe! One, two, three!"

The poor fellow was most terribly scared. I said, "Friday, we must resolve to fight them. Can you fight, Friday?" "Me shoot," says he, "but there come many great number." "No matter for that," I answered, "our guns will frighten those we do not kill."

After arming us, I took my spyglass and went up the hill to see what I could discover. There were twenty-one savages, three prisoners, and three canoes. They had landed nearer to my creek than before, where the thick wood came almost down to the sea. I came back to Friday and told him I was going to go down and kill them all, and asked him to stand by me.

I gave him one pistol and three guns. I took one pistol and the other three myself, and in this posture we set out. On the way, I began to wonder again why I intended to dip my hands in blood, to attack poor naked wretches who had neither done nor intended me any wrong, and whose barbarous customs were their own misfortune. God did not call me to be His executioner. I finally decided I would only go to watch them, and that I would act then as I felt led. Unless something directed me to do so, I would not meddle with them.

I entered the wood silently, with Friday close at my heels. I sent him to spy on them and then tell me what they were doing. He came back immediately and told me that they were all eating the flesh of one of their prisoners, and that another lay bound upon the sand to be killed next—and this was not one of their nation, but one of the bearded men who had come to their country in the boat. I was filled with horror, and going closer, I saw plainly with my spyglass a European white man with clothes on, lying on the sand with his hands and feet tied.

I sneaked forward behind bushes and trees until I was about eighty yards from them.

25
RESCUING CAPTIVES

I HAD NOT A MOMENT TO LOSE, for nineteen savages sat around the fire and had just sent two others to butcher the poor Christian and bring him to them, perhaps limb by limb. The two had stooped down to untie the captive's feet. I turned to Friday. "Now, Friday," says I, "do exactly as you see me do; fail in nothing." With a musket I took my aim at the savages, bidding him do the like. Then I asked if he was ready, and he said, "Yes." "Then fire at them," said I, and the same moment I fired.

Friday took his aim so much better than I, that on his side he killed two and wounded three, while I on my side killed one and wounded two. They were, you may be sure, in a dreadful consternation. All who were not hurt jumped up, but did not know which way to run, for they didn't know where their destruction came from. Friday watched me closely as I picked up my fowling-piece and cocked it, and he did the same. "Are you ready, Friday?" said I. "Yes," said he. "Let fly then!" and with that we fired. We were using swanshot or small pistol-bullets, and so only two dropped. But the many wounded ran about yelling and screaming like mad creatures, all bloody, and miserably wounded. Three of these fell down, not quite dead.

"Now, Friday," says I, taking up my musket which was still loaded, "follow me!" I rushed out of the wood with Friday close behind. As soon as they saw me, I shouted as loud as I could and ran as fast as I could (which, by the way, was not very fast, being loaded down with guns) and rushed toward the poor victim lying upon the beach. His two butchers had left him and fled in a terrible fright and had jumped into their canoe. I turned to Friday, and told him to fire at them. He ran about forty yards toward shore and shot at them, and they fell in a heap in the boat.

Meanwhile, I pulled out my knife, freed the poor victim, and asked him in Portuguese who he was. He answered in Latin, "Christianus," but was so weak and faint that he could scarce stand or speak. I took my bottle out of my pocket and gave it him, and I gave him a piece of bread, which he ate. Then I asked him what nationality he was; and he said, "Espagniole." "Senor," said I, with as much Spanish as I could muster, "we will talk afterwards, but we must fight now. If you have any strength left, take this pistol and sword, and lay about you." He took them very thankfully, and flew upon his murderers like a fury, and cut two of them in pieces in an instant. The truth is that the poor creatures were so frightened by the noise of our gunfire that they fell down in fear, unable to try to escape.

I sent Friday inland for the muskets we had first fired, and then I reloaded them. During this time, one of the savages attacked the Spaniard with the great wooden sword that was to have butchered him earlier. The Spaniard cut him two great wounds on his head; but the powerful savage threw him down and was wringing my sword out of his hand. The Spaniard, though underneath, wisely dropped the sword, drew his pistol, shot the savage in the chest, and killed him upon the spot.

Friday pursued others with his hatchet, and with that he finished three who had fallen down wounded. He and the Spaniard shot all they could, but one who was wounded plunged into the sea and swam with all his might out to the canoe. Those in the canoe were all that escaped. The account is as follows:

3 killed at our first shot from the tree
2 killed at the next shot
2 killed by Friday in the boat
2 killed by ditto, of those at first wounded
1 killed by ditto in the wood
3 killed by the Spaniard
4 killed by Friday, already wounded
4 escaped in the boat (one wounded, if not dead)
21 in all.

Friday wanted to pursue those in the canoe, and I was worried about their escape, lest they should come back later with two or three hundred of their canoes and overwhelm us. So I ran to one of their canoes and jumped in, with Friday following me. But there I found another poor creature bound hand and foot, awaiting slaughter, and almost dead with fear. He had not been able to look up over the side of the boat, he was tied so tightly, and had been tied so long that he had little life in him.

I immediately untied him; but he groaned pitifully, believing that he was going to be killed.

As Friday approached, I told him to inform the man that he was rescued. But when Friday looked into his face, it would have moved any one to tears to have seen how he kissed him, hugged him, cried, laughed, jumped about, danced, sang, then cried again, then jumped about again, like a crazy creature. It was a long time before I could make him tell me what was the matter; but when he could control himself, he told me it was his father.

It is not easy for me to tell about the ecstasy of affection this poor savage felt at the sight of his father and his father's rescue. He went in and out of the boat a great many times. He rubbed his father's arms and ankles which were stiff and numb, and held his father close.

That was the end of our pursuit of the canoe with the other savages, and it was fortunate for us that we did not follow them—for within two hours, before they could have got a quarter of the way home, a great wind came up against them and blew all night, so at the time I doubted whether they ever reached their own coast.

But to return to Friday. I asked him if he had given his father any bread. He shook his head, and said, "None; ugly dog eat all up self." So I gave him a cake of bread and two or three bunches of raisins for his father. He had no sooner given these to his father than I saw him come out of the boat and run away, as if he had been bewitched, he ran so fast; for he was the swiftest runner that I ever saw. In a quarter of an hour I saw him come back again, though not so fast as he went.

He had gone home for an earthen jug of fresh water, and had got two more little loaves of bread. The bread he gave me, but the water he carried to his father. However, as I was very thirsty too, I took a little sip of it. This water revived his father, for he had been fainting with thirst.

When his father had drunk, I told Friday to give some water and bread to the poor Spaniard, who needed it as much as his father. The man was lying upon a green place under the shade of a tree, and his arms and legs were swollen from having been tied. I went to him with a handful of raisins. He looked up at me with all the gratitude and thankfulness that a face could hold, but he could not stand up upon his feet although he tried to do it two or three times. So I told Friday to rub his ankles, as he had done his father's.

While caring for the Spaniard, Friday turned to see his father every two or three minutes. One time his father had disappeared, and without speaking a word he ran to him so fast that one could scarce see his feet touch the ground. When he got there, he found that his father had lain down to ease his legs. A little later, Friday lifted the Spaniard up upon his back, carried him to the boat, and set him down close to his father. Then he launched the boat and paddled it along the shore faster than I could walk, though the wind blew pretty hard. So he brought them into our creek.

160

I quickly made a kind of hand-barrow for them, and Friday and I carried them up both together upon it between us. But when we got them to the outside of our wall, we were at a loss, for it was impossible to get them over, and I was determined not to break it down. So I set to work again, and in about two hours' time, Friday and I made a very handsome tent, covered with old sails, and above that with boughs. Here we made two beds of good rice-straw, with blankets laid upon it to lie on, and another to cover them, on each bed.

My island was now richly populated, and I thought merrily how like a king I was. First of all, the whole country was my own property. Secondly, my people were perfect citizens. I was absolute lord and lawgiver; they all owed their lives to me and were ready to lay down their lives for me. It was remarkable, too, that my three subjects were of three different religions. My man Friday was a Protestant, his father was a pagan cannibal, and the Spaniard was a Roman Catholic. However, I allowed freedom of religion throughout my kingdom. But this is by the way.

The first thing I did when my guests were settled down was to order Friday to kill a yearling goat from my flock. I chopped the hindquarter into small pieces and set Friday to work boiling and stewing, and made them a very good dish with barley and rice in the broth. Having set a table in their tent for them, I sat down and ate my own dinner with them, and as well as I could cheered them, and encouraged them. Friday was my interpreter to both of them, for the Spaniard spoke the language of the savages pretty well.

After we had supped, I ordered Friday to take a canoe and fetch our firearms, which we had left at the place of battle. The next day I ordered him to bury the dead bodies, which lay in the sun and would soon be offensive. I also ordered him to bury the horrid remains of their feast, and which I could not bear to see. He removed all signs of the savages ever being there, so that when I went there again I could scarce recognize the place.

161

I had Friday ask his father whether we might expect a return of the savages. In his opinion they were drowned or cast ashore to the south, where they would be devoured. But if they survived, it was his opinion that they would tell their people the rest were killed by thunder and lightning, not by the hand of man, and that Friday and I were two spirits, not men with weapons. It was impossible for them to imagine that a man could dart fire, and speak thunder, and kill at a distance without lifting up the hand. And he was right—for I heard later that the savages did survive, and believed that whoever went to that enchanted island would be destroyed with fire from the gods.

Not knowing this, I was always on guard with my new army. The four of us could have beat a hundred of them.

But no more canoes appeared, and Friday's father assured me that I would be treated well in his nation, on his account.

The Spaniard told me there were sixteen more like him living at peace with the savages, but it was a hard life. I learned they were a Spanish ship bound from the Rio de la Plata to Havana with hides and silver, aiming to bring back whatever European goods they could get there. They had five Portuguese seamen on board they had saved from another wreck; five of their men were drowned when the ship was lost, and they finally arrived, almost starved, on the coast where they expected to be eaten.

I asked him if they had a plan for escape, and he said they had many meetings about it. But having no boat or tools to build one, or provisions of any kind, their meetings always ended in tears and despair.

I told him I was sure that if they were all here, we might build a boat and sail south to the Brazils or north to New Spain. But I feared to put my life into their hands, for gratitude isn't inborn in men, and they aren't all square dealers. They often act according to their own best interests instead of according to what they owe a helper. If I helped them to escape, they might make me their prisoner in New Spain, where an Englishman was certain to get killed. I would rather be caught by savages, and eaten alive, than to be betrayed for my kindness and make my case worse than before.

He answered that they were so miserable that they would abhor the thought of mistreating a helper. If I pleased, he would go to them with the old man to discuss it, and return with their answer. He would require their solemn oath that they should be absolutely under my leading as their commander and captain, and they would swear upon the holy sacraments and the gospel to go to a Christian country that I should agree to and no other. He would bring a contract from them.

Then he told me he would first swear to me himself, that he would never stir from me till I gave him orders, and that he would take my side to the last drop of his blood.

He told me they were all honest men, under the greatest distress imaginable, having no weapons or clothes, or food, and at the mercy of the savages, without hope of ever returning to their own country. He was sure that if I would rescue them they would live and die for me.

I decided to send the old savage and this Spaniard over to them, but the Spaniard pointed out that the barley and rice which was more than sufficient for myself, but barely enough for my new family of four, would not be enough for his fourteen friends, especially on a voyage. He thought we should plant more grain and wait for another harvest so they would not become bitter because of hunger. "You know," he said, "the children of Israel, though they rejoiced at first for their being freed from Egypt, were angry at God Himself, who freed them, when they got hungry in the wilderness."

So in about a month, at seed-time, we sowed twenty-two bushels of barley and sixteen jars of rice. That was more seed than we had to spare, for we didn't leave ourselves enough barley for our own food for the six months that we had to wait.

We went freely all over the island. I marked out several trees which I thought fit for our work, and I set Friday and his father to cutting them down while I had the Spaniard oversee their work. I showed

163

them how I had hewed a large tree into single planks, and I caused them to make about a dozen large planks of good oak, nearly two feet broad, thirty-five feet long, and from two inches to four inches thick.

I increased my little flock of tame goats as much as I could, catching about twenty wild young kids to breed with the rest. I dried a prodigious quantity of grapes in the sun, an extremely nourishing food.

At harvest, from our twenty-two bushels of barley we thrashed out above two hundred and twenty bushels, with a similar gain in rice. That was enough for sixteen Spaniards on shore or at sea. We made great baskets, in which we kept it.

Now ready for all the guests I expected, I sent the Spaniard to the mainland for those he had left behind. With strict instructions, he and Friday's father went away in one of the canoes in which they were brought when they came as prisoners to be devoured by the savages. I gave each of them a musket, with a firelock on it, and about eight charges of powder and ball, charging them not to use either of them except in an emergency.

I gave them enough bread and dried grapes to last them many days, and to last the rest for about eight days' time. Wishing them a good voyage, I saw them go.

They went away with a fair gale on the day that the moon was at full, by my calendar in the month of October. But I had lost track of the exact days on my calendar long ago.

Eight days later, a strange accident intervened, the likes of which has probably never been heard of. I was fast asleep in my hutch one morning, when my man Friday came running to me, and called aloud, "Master, master, they are come, they are come."

I jumped up and rushed out as soon as I could get my clothes on. Turning my eyes to the sea, I saw a boat about a league and a half away heading for shore, with what they call a shoulder-of-mutton sail. I called Friday in, for these were not the people we waited for, and we didn't know yet whether they were friends or enemies.

Next, I fetched my spyglass, and climbed up to the top of the hill. I discovered a ship lying at an anchor at about two leagues and a half from me, south-south-east. It appeared to be an English ship, and the boat appeared to be an English longboat.

The joy of seeing a ship, and one who I had reason to believe was manned by my own countrymen, and consequently friends, was such as I cannot describe. But some secret doubts told me to keep up my guard. An English ship had no business in that part of the world and I knew there had been no storms to drive them here; and so if they were English, they were probably here for no good purpose. I would rather continue as I was than fall into the hands of thieves and murderers.

Let no man despise the secret hints of danger which sometimes are given him when he may think there is no possibility of its being real. That such hints and notices are given us, few observant people can deny. If I had not been made cautious by this secret hint, I would have ended in far worse condition than before, as you will see presently.

I saw the boat draw near the shore, as if they looked for a creek to thrust in at for the convenience of landing. However, they did not see my little inlet, but landed upon the beach—which was fortunate. Otherwise, they would have landed almost at my door, and might have plundered me.

There were eleven men, and three of them were prisoners. One of the three was obviously begging and despairing, and the other two appeared concerned indeed, but not so wildly upset.

I was bewildered. Friday called out to me in English as well as he could, "O master! You see English mans eat prisoner as well as savage mans." "No, no," says I, "Friday, I am afraid they will murder them, indeed, but you may be sure they will not eat them." All this while I had no thought of what the matter really was, but stood trembling with the horror of the sight, expecting every moment that the three prisoners should be killed. All the blood in my body seemed to run chill in my veins.

I saw the insolent seamen run scattering about the land, as if they wanted to see the country. The three other men were free to go also, but they sat down in despair. This reminded me of my own first day and night on shore. As I knew nothing that night of the supplies I would receive from the ship coming closer, so these three poor desolate men knew nothing of how near their help and safety was.

So it is that we have reason to depend cheerfully upon the great Maker of the world, who even in the worst circumstances, gives his creatures something to be thankful for. Sometimes help is nearer than we imagine, and we are rescued by what threatens to destroy us.

26
THE MUTINEERS

THESE PEOPLE HAD COME ASHORE at high tide. While they rambled around, the tide went out and left their boat aground.

They had left two men in the boat, who, as I found out afterwards, drank a little too much brandy and fell asleep. When one awoke and found the boat stuck, he yelled for the rest, who were straggling about, and they all came back. But the boat was too heavy for them to move, and the shore on that side was a soft oozy sand, almost like a quicksand.

Like true seamen, who seem to do less planning ahead than the rest of mankind, they gave up and strolled away again. I heard one of them call to another, "Forget it, Jack! She will float next tide." That proved which country they were from.

I didn't dare to stir out of my castle any farther than to the top of the hill. I knew it was ten hours before the boat could float again, and by that time it would be dark, when I could do something. In the meantime, I prepared Friday and myself for battle. I looked very fierce. I had my goat-skin coat on, with the great cap I have mentioned, a naked sword by my side, two pistols in my belt, and a gun upon each shoulder.

I planned to wait for dark, but about two o'clock, in the heat of the day, I found that they had all gone straggling into the wood to go to sleep. The three prisoners, too frightened to get any sleep, were under a great tree about a quarter of a mile from me, and out of sight of the rest.

I decided to reveal myself to them. I sneaked as close as I could, and then, before any of them saw me, I called aloud in Spanish, "Who are you, gentlemen?"

They jumped at the noise, but were ten times more surprised when they saw me. They looked ready to run, so I spoke to them in English. "Gentlemen," said I, "perhaps you have a friend near you when you did not expect it." "He must be sent directly from heaven then," said one of them very gravely, "for our condition is past the help of man." "All help is from heaven, sir," said I. "But can you tell a stranger how to help you? I saw you when you landed; and when you seemed to beg the brutes that came with you, I saw one of them threaten to kill you with his sword."

The poor man, with tears running down his face and trembling, replied, "Am I talking to God, or man? Is it a real man, or an angel?" "Be in no fear about that, sir," said I. "If God had sent an angel, he would have come better clothed, with different weapons. Pray lay aside your fears; I am a man, an Englishman, and eager to help you. I have one servant and we have arms and ammunition. Tell us freely, can we serve you? What is your trouble?"

"Our trouble," said he, "is too long to tell while our murderers are so near; but in short, sir, I was commander of that ship. My men have mutinied, have almost murdered me, and put me on shore in this desolate place with these two men—my mate and a passenger. We expected to perish, believing the place to be uninhabited."

"Do you know where they are gone?" I asked. "There they lie, sir," said he, pointing to a thicket of trees. "If they have heard you, they will certainly murder us all."

"Have they any firearms?" said I. He answered, "They have only two guns, and one left in the boat." "Well then," said I, "leave the rest to me. Shall we kill them or take them prisoners?" He told me that except for two desperate villains, he believed all the rest would return to their duty. So we went away quietly to make our plans.

"Look, sir," said I, "if I try to rescue you, are you willing to make two promises to me? 1. That while you stay on this island with me, you will be governed entirely by my orders. 2. That if the ship is recovered, you will carry me and my man to England, passage free."

He gave me every assurance that he would comply with these reasonable demands. And besides, would owe his life to me and say so as long as he lived.

"Well then," said I, "here are three muskets for you, with powder and ball." I told him the best method I could think of was to fire upon the traitors at once, as they lay. If any was not killed at the first volley, and surrendered, we might save them, and so put it wholly upon God's providence to direct the shot.

He said he didn't want to kill them if he could help it, but if the two evil ones who led the mutiny escaped, we should be undone, for they would go back to the ship and bring the whole crew with them and destroy us all. However, he was still cautious about shedding blood, and I told him to manage the attack.

We heard some of them awaken, and two of them got up. He said they were not the leaders of the mutiny, so I said, "You may let them escape because Providence seems to have wakened them. But if the rest escape, it is your fault."

With that, he took the musket I had given him, and he and his two companions began to advance. The two men accompanying him accidentally made some noise, and one of the seamen saw him and cried out to the rest; but the moment he cried out, the two men fired. They had aimed so well that one of the mutineers was killed on the spot, and the other badly wounded. He struggled up and called for help. But the captain told him it was too late to cry for help, he should call upon God to forgive him. With that he knocked him down with the stock of his musket, so that he never spoke again. When the men saw that it was vain to resist, they begged for mercy. The captain told them he would spare their lives if they would swear to be faithful to him while he was recovering the ship, and they agreed. I was not against that, but I ordered him to keep them bound hand and foot while they were on the island.

I sent Friday with the captain's mate to the boat, to bring away the oars and sail, which they did. By and by three straggling men, who were (fortunately for them) napping elsewhere, came back. Seeing their captain, who had been their prisoner, now their conqueror, they surrendered, and so our victory was complete.

Now the captain and I could get acquainted. I told him my whole history, which he heard with amazement, particularly the wonderful manner of my being furnished with provisions and ammunition. Indeed, as my story is a whole collection of wonders, it moved him deeply. But when he thought about himself, and how I seemed to have been preserved there on purpose to save his life, the tears ran down his face and he could not speak.

After this, I took him and his two men into my apartment, where I refreshed them with such provisions as I had, and showed them all the contrivances I had made during my long, long life there.

Above all, the captain admired my fortification, and how perfectly I had concealed it with a grove of trees, impassable except for my little winding path. I told him this was my castle, but that I had a country home, as most princes have, and I would show him that at another time. At present, our business was to consider how to recover the ship. He told me there were still twenty-six hands on board who would be desperate, knowing that the penalty for mutiny would be the gallows as soon as they came to England or to any of the English colonies.

It occurred to me that in a little while the ship's crew would certainly come on shore in the other boat to search for their lost crew members.

The first thing we had to do was to damage the boat on the beach, so that they couldn't carry her off. Accordingly, we went on board, took the firearms, a bottle of brandy and another of rum, a few biscuit-cakes, a horn of gunpowder, and a five-or-six pound lump of sugar in a piece of canvas.

When we had carried all these things on shore (the oars, mast, sail, and rudder of the boat were carried away before), we knocked a great hole in her bottom so they couldn't take her. My plan was that if they left us the boat, I could fix her and carry us away to the Leeward Islands, and call upon our friends the Spaniards on my way, for I had them still in my thoughts.

We had by brute strength heaved the broken boat up on the beach so high that the tide would not float her off at high-watermark, when we heard the distant ship fire a gun, and saw her raise her flag as a signal for the boat to return. But no boat stirred.

At last, when all their signals and firings proved fruitless, we saw them hoist another boat out and row towards the shore. There were ten armed men in her. As she approached, the captain saw that there were three very honest fellows in her, who must have been overpowered and frightened into joining the mutiny. The others were dangerous and he feared them.

I smiled at him, and told him that men in our circumstances were beyond fear. "And where, sir," said I, "is your belief that I was preserved here to save your life, the belief that made you so joyful a little while ago? Every man that comes ashore is in our hands, and shall die or live according to how they behave to us." As I said this loudly with a cheerful face, it greatly encouraged him.

We had sent two untrustworthy prisoners to my cave for safekeeping. They were bound, but had provisions and candles. We promised them that if they remained there quietly, we would set them free in a day or two; but if they tried to escape, they would be put to death without mercy.

Two of the other prisoners were kept bound, but the other two became our helpers upon their solemnly promising to live and die with us. With them and the ex-prisoners we were seven armed men. I didn't doubt we could handle the ten that were coming.

They ran their boat up onto the beach, and all came on shore. The first thing they did was to run to their other boat. They were shocked to find her stripped empty, with a great hole in her bottom. They began calling with all their might to their missing companions, to no avail. Then they fired their guns, and the echoes made the woods ring. But the men in the cave could not hear, and the others didn't dare to answer.

They decided to go right back to their ship and report that the men were all murdered. Accordingly, they immediately launched their boat again and got on board. The captain was confounded, believing they gave up their comrades for lost and would sail away in his ship.

But they changed their minds and returned to shore again. This time they left three men in the boat a good distance from shore while the rest went to look for their companions. Now we were at a loss, for if we seized those seven men on shore, the other three would row away to the ship and set sail. However, we had no remedy but to wait and see.

Those that came on shore kept close together, hiking toward the top of the little hill above my castle. We could see them plainly, though they could not see us. At the top, they shouted and called till they were weary, obviously not willing to venture far from the shore or from one another. Then they sat down together under a tree to talk.

The captain suggested that if they all fired their guns as a signal, and if we attacked before they could reload, they would surrender without bloodshed.

But this event did not happen. We waited a great while, and they finally got up and hiked back toward the sea. It seems they were so frightened that they decided to give up on their lost companions and continue their intended voyage with the ship.

Then I thought of a trick to fetch them back again, which fit my purpose to a T. I ordered Friday and the captain's mate to hurry over the little creek westward about half a mile. There they were to call as loud as they could. As soon as they heard the seamen answer them, they should call again, then keep out of sight, move along, always answering when called, to lure them as far inland into the woods as possible. Then they were to return to me as I directed them.

As the men were getting into their boat, Friday and the mate called. The men answered and ran along the shore westward, toward the voice they heard—but they were stopped by the high tide in the creek and called for their boat to come up the creek and carry them across, as I had expected.

The boat came a good way up into the creek, and one of the three men got out to go along with the others, leaving only two in the boat. They fastened her to the stump of a little tree on the shore.

That was just what I wanted. Leaving Friday and the captain's mate to their task, we surprised the two men before they were aware. The fellow on shore was half asleep when the captain knocked him down and yelled at the one in the boat to yield, or he was a dead man.

It took little argument to persuade him to yield when he saw five men coming at him, and his comrade knocked down. Besides, he was one who didn't like the mutiny and was easily persuaded to join us.

In the meantime, Friday and the captain's mate drew the others from one hill to another, and from one wood to another, till they were sure they could not return to the boat before dark.

It was several hours after Friday came back to me before the men got back to their boat. We could hear the fastest one calling to those behind to hurry, and could hear the rest complain how lame and tired they were.

It is impossible to describe their confusion when they found the boat fast aground in the creek, now that the tide was out, and their two men gone. They started telling one another they were on an enchanted island, that either there were people on it and they would be murdered, or else there were devils and spirits on it, and they would be carried away and devoured.

They called their two comrades' names many times, but got no answer. We could see them run about in despair, sit down in the boat to rest themselves, then walk about again, and so the same thing over again.

I was willing to wait in order to kill as few of them as I could. I was unwilling to risk the killing of any of our own men. I hoped that they would separate, and we crept closer.

Then the boatswain, who was the principal ringleader of the mutiny, came walking along with two more of their crew. The captain could hardly wait. When they came nearer, the captain and Friday jumped to their feet and shot them.

The boatswain was killed upon the spot. The next man fell right by him and died an hour or two later. The third ran for it.

At the noise of the gunfire I immediately advanced with my whole army, which was now eight men: myself, generalissimo; Friday, my lieutenant-general; the captain and his two men, and the three prisoners of war, whom we had armed.

In the dark they couldn't see our number, so I made the man we had spared in the boat, who was now one of us, call to them by name. So he called out as loud as he could, "Tom Smith! Tom Smith!" Tom Smith knew his voice and answered, "Who's that? Robinson?" He answered, "Yes; for God's sake, Tom, throw down your arms and surrender, or you are all dead men."

"Who? Where are they?" says Smith again. "Here they are," says Robinson. "Here's our captain, and fifty men with him, hunting you for two hours. The boatswain is killed, Will Frye is wounded, and I am a prisoner; and if you do not yield, you are all lost."

"Will they give us mercy then?" says Tom Smith. "I'll go and ask, if

174

you promise to surrender," says Robinson. So the captain then calls out, "You, Smith, you know my voice. If you lay down your arms immediately and submit, I'll spare your lives—all but Will Atkins."

27
HEADING HOME

AT THIS WILL ATKINS CRIED OUT, "For God's sake, captain, what have I done? I'm no worse than the rest"—which was not true, for it seems Will Atkins had abused the captain the worst. In answer, the captain told him to appeal to the governor—by which he meant me, for they all called me governor.

They all laid down their arms and begged for their lives. Three of my men bound them all, and then my great army of fifty men, which really came to exactly eight, seized their boat. But I kept myself out of sight for reasons of state.

Our next work was to repair the boat, and think of seizing the ship. As for the captain, now he had leisure to parley with them, he expostulated with them upon the villainy of their practices with him, and at length upon the farther wickedness of their design, and how certainly it must bring them to misery and distress in the end, and perhaps to the gallows.

They all appeared very penitent, and begged for their lives. The captain told them they were not his prisoners, but the commander of the island. They had meant to set him on shore in a barren, uninhabited island, but God had directed them to an island that was inhabited. The governor was an Englishman who could hang them all there, if he pleased. But he would probably send them to England to be sentenced—except Atkins, who should prepare for death, because the governor intended to have him hanged in the morning.

Though this was all a fiction of his own, it had its desired effect. Atkins fell to his knees to beg the captain to try to change the governor's mind, and all the rest begged not be sent to England.

It now occurred to me that the time of our deliverance had come, and that it would be easy to recruit these fellows to help us get the ship, so I stayed hidden in the dark and called the captain as if from a distance. One of the men was ordered to say to the captain, "Captain, the commander calls for you," and the captain replied, "Tell his excellency I am coming." This impressed them, and they all believed that the commander was waiting with his fifty men.

When the captain came to me, I told him my plan for seizing the ship, which he liked wonderfully well. I told him we must divide the prisoners, and that we should imprison Atkins and two more of the worst of them in my cave.

Friday and two others took them to the cave prison. The others were tied and imprisoned in my country home. In the morning the captain told them that if they were sent to England they would all be hanged in chains, to be sure. But if they would join his attempt as to recover the ship, he would have the governor pardon them.

They fell down on their knees and promised, with the deepest vows, that they would be faithful to him to the last drop, and that they would owe their lives to him and follow him anywhere, that they would consider him a father to them as long as they lived.

"Well," says the captain, "I must go and tell the governor what you say, and see if I can get him to agree."

For our safety, I told him to go back and choose five of them to be his assistants, saying that the governor would keep the remaining five as hostages. If his assistants were unfaithful, the five hostages would be hanged in chains alive upon the shore.

This convinced them that the governor was in earnest. They had no choice but to accept it. By now it was the wish of the hostages, as much as the captain, to persuade the other five to do their duty.

This was our crew: 1. The captain, his mate, and passenger. 2. The two prisoners from the first gang. 3. The other two whom I released from my country home. 4. The newly released five. They were twelve in all, besides the five we kept prisoners in the cave for hostages.

I asked the captain if he was willing to venture with this crew on board the ship. I did not think it was proper for me and my man Friday to go, for it was enough for us to keep the seven prisoners guarded and supplied with food. As for the five in the cave, Friday went in twice a day to supply their needs.

The captain told the two hostages I was the person the governor had ordered to look after them, and that they could not stir anywhere unless I said so. If they did, they would be dragged to the castle and chained. Since they had never seen me as governor, I now appeared as another person. I frequently spoke of the governor, the garrison, the castle, and the like.

The captain now prepared his two boats, and they approached the ship about midnight. As soon as they came within call of the ship, he made his man Robinson call to them, saying they had found the men and the boat but that it had taken a long time, and the like, holding them in conversation till they came to the ship's side. Then the captain and the mate boarded the ship and knocked down the second mate and carpenter with the butt-end of their muskets. They tied all the men on the main and quarter-decks, and began to fasten the hatches to keep down those below deck. The men from the other boat seized the forecastle and the scuttle which went down into the kitchen, capturing the three men they found there.

When this was done, and all safe on deck, the captain ordered the mate and three men to break into the round-house, where the mutineers' captain had awakened and armed himself. When the mate split open the door with a crowbar, the new captain and his men fired at

179

them, breaking the mate's arm with a musket-ball, and they wounded two others, but killed nobody.

The mate rushed into the round-house, wounded as he was, and shot the mutineers' captain through the head. The bullet entered at his mouth and came out again behind one of his ears, so that he never spoke a word. At that, the rest surrendered and the ship was taken with no more lives lost. The captain ordered seven guns fired to signal his success, which you may be sure I was very glad to hear after waiting for it till nearly two in the morning.

Knowing that all was well, I lay down and slept soundly till I was startled by the noise of a gun. Then I heard a man call me by the name of "Governor, Governor," and recognized the captain's voice. There he stood at the top of my hill, pointing to the ship. "My dear friend and deliverer," says he, "there's your ship, for she is all yours, and so are we, and all that belong to her." I cast my eyes to the ship, and there she rode within little more than half mile of the shore, for they had lifted her anchor and brought her near.

I was ready to pass out, for I saw my rescue right there in my hands, everything easy, and a large ship ready to carry me wherever I pleased to go. I wasn't able to answer him one word. If he hadn't been hugging me, I would have fallen to the ground.

He saw that I was faint and pulled a bottle out of his pocket to give me a swallow of sweet cordial. After I drank it, I sat down upon the ground. Though it cleared my head, yet it was a long time before I could speak. All this while the poor man was in as great an ecstasy as I, and he said a thousand kind things to help me get hold of myself. But I was so flooded with joy that I was struck dumb. At last I broke out into tears, and after that I could talk again.

I told him I looked upon him as a man sent from heaven to deliver me, and that the whole transaction seemed to be a chain of wonders. Such things show that we have a secret hand of Providence governing the world. I didn't forget to lift up my heart in thankfulness to heaven, for what heart could fail to bless Him who causes every rescue?

When we had talked awhile, the captain had his men bring me gifts of food and drink as if I were staying on the island instead of leaving soon. What was a thousand times more useful to me than the food, he brought me six clean new shirts, six very good neckcloths, two pair of gloves, one pair of shoes and stockings, a hat, and a very good suit of his own that was almost new. In a word, he clothed me from head to foot. I was delighted, but when I put the clothes on I found them very uncomfortable at first.

We began to consider what to do with our prisoners. Two of them were such rogues that if he did carry them away, they must be in chains to be delivered over to justice at the first English colony he came to.

I told him that if he desired it, I could probably get the two men to request that we leave them on the island. "With all my heart," said the captain. So I caused Friday and a couple of helpers to bring the five prisoners from the cave to my country home to await me.

After some time, I arrived in my new governor's clothes. I told the prisoners I had a full account of their villainous behavior to the captain, and how they had run away with the ship, and were planning further robberies, but that they had fallen into the pit which they had dug for others.

I let them know that I had seized the ship and that they would soon see their false captain hanging on the yard-arm. As for them, I wanted to know any reason why I should not formally execute them as pirates.

They answered that when they surrendered they had been offered mercy. But I told them I knew of no way to grant mercy, because I and my men were leaving the island to sail for England, and in England they would be hanged at the gallows for mutiny. The only alternative was for me to leave them on the island if they preferred it.

They said they would much rather stay there than to be carried to

England to be hanged. The captain pretended that he didn't want to leave them there, but I acted a little angry and told him they were my prisoners, not his. If he didn't consent to my plan, I would set them free, and then it would be up to him to catch them again on his own.

When they had all declared their willingness to stay, I gave them the whole history of the place and of my coming to it. I showed them my fortifications, the way I made my bread, planted my grain, and dried my grapes. I left them my firearms, swords, and gunpowder. I gave them a description of the way I managed the goats, and directions to milk and fatten them, and to make both butter and cheese. I gave them my new garden seeds, which I wished I had had earlier. Also I gave them the bag of peas which the captain had given me, and told them be sure to plant them.

I told them also about the sixteen Spaniards that were expected, for whom I left a letter of explanation, and made them promise to treat the Spaniards well.

The next day I went on board the ship. The next morning early two of the five men came swimming to the ship's side and begged to be taken into the ship before they were murdered by the other three. We finally allowed them on board. After they were soundly whipped they proved very honest and quiet fellows from then on.

When the tide came up, the captain sent to the three men on shore their chests and clothes, which they were very thankful for. I also encouraged them by telling them that if I had the chance to send any vessel to pick them up, I would not forget them.

When I left the island, I carried on board for keepsakes the great goatskin cap I had made, my umbrella, and my parrot. I didn't forget the money, which had grown tarnished and could hardly pass for silver till it had been polished, and also the money I found in the wreck of the Spanish ship.

And thus I left the island the 19th of December, as I learned from the ship's records, in the year 1686, after I had been there twenty-eight

And thus I left the island . . . after I had been there
twenty-eight years, two months, and nineteen days . . .

years, two months, and nineteen days—escaping from this second captivity the same day of the month that I first made my escape from the Moors of Sallee.

In this vessel, after a long voyage, I arrived in England on the 11th of June in the year 1687, having been thirty-five years absent.

Although most modern editions of *Robinson Crusoe* end here, the story isn't really over. Back in England, Crusoe, accompanied by Friday, finds that his family is all dead except for two sisters and two nephews. Traveling to Lisbon, Portugal, he locates his old friend the captain and learns that the plantation in Brazil has prospered greatly. When his honest Brazilian partner learns that Crusoe is still alive, he sends him his share of the fortune. Then Crusoe, Friday, and some friends head toward England on horseback, through a wolf-infested part of Spain and on into France. Safely back in England at last, Crusoe marries happily and becomes a gentleman farmer with three children; but he is still obsessed with his island. After his young wife dies, he sails away with his nephew in January 1695 for further adventures.

So it is that seven years after their escape, Crusoe and Friday return to their island with gifts and supplies. They find that the shipwrecked Spaniards who arrived from the mainland long ago have been managing and defending the island well. They have also obtained wives from the mainland and have several children already. Will Atkins has become an earnest Christian. After three weeks on the island, Crusoe's ship sails to Brazil and Friday is killed. The ship sails down around the tip of South America, then on to Madagascar and China—where the rebellious crew sets Crusoe ashore. He has adventures in Southeast Asia and eventually makes his way through China, Siberia, and Russia. After this amazing ten-year trip around the world, Crusoe arrives back in England on January 10, 1705.

Robinson Crusoe ends his life story looking forward to heaven: "And here I resolved to prepare for a longer journey than all these, having lived a life of infinite variety seventy-two years, and learned the blessing of ending our days in peace."

About the author and *Robinson Crusoe*

Daniel Defoe (1660–1731) traveled a great deal, served as a soldier, sold ship insurance, succeeded in the hosiery business, failed in the brick business, and worked as a political secret agent. But his main career was journalism. To support his wife and six children, he wrote over 560 books, pamphlets, and papers. On a couple of occasions his peppery prose landed him in prison for embarrassing people in power.

Defoe was almost sixty years old when he finally turned to fiction. A Scottish sailor's real-life adventures inspired him to write *Robinson Crusoe* (1719), which was an instant bestseller. In his last ten years, Defoe quickly wrote seven more novels, as well as more nonfiction books. But *Robinson Crusoe* is the favorite and always will be.

***

"*Robinson Crusoe* is read as eagerly today as when it was first published. . . . The book has attained a high place in the literature of the world, and justly so."—*Masterplots.*

About the editor

Kathryn Lindskoog, an educator, literary critic, and expert on C. S. Lewis, has written more than twenty books. Among them are *C. S. Lewis: Mere Christian*; *A Child's Garden of Christian Verses* and *How to Grow a Young Reader.* She earned her B.A. at the University of Redlands and her M.A. at California State University at Long Beach. In addition to teaching high-school English for seven years, she has taught as an adjunct instructor at Seattle Pacific University, Biola University, New Orleans Baptist Seminary, and Fuller Theological Seminary. Her teaching career has been limited by multiple sclerosis, which became disabling in the 1960s. Lindskoog is married with two grown sons. She lives in Orange, California.

About the illustrator

Barbara Chitouras has been a freelance artist for almost twenty years, creating artwork for children's books, textbooks, and rubber stamp designs. She studied at Massachusetts College of Art in Boston and has a B.A. in Illustration. She currently lives in the Boston area.